MARGIE KELLY
BREAKS
THE DRESS CODE

MARGIE KELLY BREAKS THE DRESS CODE

BRIDGET FARR

LITTLE, BROWN AND COMPANY
New York   Boston

Little, Brown and Company
Hachette Book Group
1290 Avenue of the Americas, New York, NY 10104
Visit us at LBYR.com

First Edition: July 2021

Little, Brown and Company is a division of Hachette Book Group, Inc. The Little, Brown name and logo are trademarks of Hachette Book Group, Inc.

The publisher is not responsible for websites (or their content) that are not owned by the publisher.

Library of Congress Cataloging-in-Publication Data
Names: Farr, Bridget, author.
Title: Margie Kelly breaks the dress code / by Bridget Farr.
Description: First edition. | New York : Little, Brown and Company, 2021. | Audience: Ages 8–12. | Summary: After her first day of middle school is ruined by a dress code violation, Margie Kelly begins to notice blatant sexism and decides to protest the school's gender inequality.
Identifiers: LCCN 2020048833 | ISBN 9780316461573 (hardcover) | ISBN 9780316461566 (ebook) | ISBN 9780316461559 (ebook other)
Subjects: CYAC: Middle schools—Fiction. | Schools—Fiction. | Protest movements—Fiction. | Dress codes—Fiction. | Fathers and daughters—Fiction.
Classification: LCC PZ7.1.F3678 Mar 2021 | DDC [Fic]—dc23
LC record available at https://lccn.loc.gov/2020048833

ISBNs: 978-0-316-46157-3 (hardcover), 978-0-316-46156-6 (ebook)

Printed in the United States of America

LSC-C

Printing 1, 2021

For my parents—
just by listening, you showed
me I had something to say

chapter 1

CLOTHING DOES **NOT** DEFINE US.

A scuffed wooden ruler with worn black numbers waits right between my eyes. Maybe Ms. Scott is going to rap my knuckles with it like I saw in one of the old movies Dad likes to watch on rainy days. That wrinkled teacher had tiny rectangular glasses at the end of her pointy nose and a really high bun at the top of her head, her hair wrapped up tight like the detonator to her dynamite. Her lips were pursed in a tight coil, the ruler in her hands ready to strike. Even though Ms. Scott looks like she could still be in college, she has the same rectangular glasses and high bun, so at the moment I'm panicking. I didn't think teachers could do that anymore: whack your hands with a ruler. And I didn't even do anything wrong! I've been in sixth grade for literally five minutes. I hadn't even finished writing my last name, Kelly, on my handout.

I've followed all the rules since I came to this pale-blue classroom. I even got here a few minutes early, skipping the huge line at the water fountain so I wouldn't be late. I went straight to the desk with my name on it and didn't even try to switch the sticker so I could sit next to my best friend, Daniela, even though I saw a boy in the back row do it so he could sit next to his best friend. I didn't smile or wave at the few other kids I recognized from elementary, either. I wrote my name only after Ms. Scott told us to start. And in print because my cursive isn't that great. We barely practiced it last year.

I answered the silly "Would you rather..." questions she had on the board: "Would you rather have an elephant trunk or a giraffe's neck?" Giraffe neck.

"Would you rather wear clown shoes every day or a clown wig?" Clown shoes.

Would you rather stand behind your teacher's desk while she holds a ruler in front of your face or show up to the first day of middle school wearing a diaper?

Diaper all the way.

Okay, probably not.

But I really wish she didn't have that ruler in her hand.

"Margaret, did your family get a copy of the handbook at orientation?" Ms. Scott asks, resting the ruler on her denim skirt. Behind me pencils scratch as people finish their "Would you rather..." questions, the timer counting down the minutes until they're ready to stare at me.

"I think so. My dad took all the papers."

She smiles. "Okay. Well, he'll need to look at it again, so he can review the dress code. Your skirt is out of compliance."

I look down at the three perfect navy tulle tiers in my first-day-of-school skirt, each layer trimmed in sequins that swing when I walk. Last week when Dad and I went shopping at the Lone Star Mall, we had the skirt-versus-leggings discussion and how Texas is too hot in August for anything but a skirt. I didn't want anything too princess-cupcake, but I couldn't resist the shimmer of the purple and turquoise sequins. The skirt was perfect, like a chocolate-dipped Oreo. I run my hand along the bottom ruffle.

"I need to measure your skirt real quick, and then we can send you to the office to change if my assumption is correct. But I'm never wrong about this."

Dad thought this skirt was perfect. Just like me. Just like my first day of middle school should be. Turns out Dad was wrong.

I flash a look over my shoulder to see if anyone is watching. Every head is down except for Daniela, who is looking at me as if her eyes are going to pop out of her head. "Are you okay?" she mouths. I snap my head around. Please don't cry.

"Whew, it's hot in here," Ms. Scott says, her pale cheeks flushed red. She wipes a drip of sweat from her hairline before turning to the class. "You have two minutes to finish that warm-up, so we can start to get to know each other," she calls. "It's your first official assignment of sixth grade!" She whispers to me, "If you'll just turn around quick, I have to measure from the back of the center of your leg."

I slowly turn around, trying to find where to look. The clock? The "Classroom Expectations" poster written in Ms. Scott's perfect teacher handwriting? Daniela? Definitely not Daniela. If I make eye contact, I will totally cry, and I cannot cry on the first day of middle school. The ruler feels cool against my skin.

"Yep. Exactly what I thought. Five and a quarter inches. Over an inch too short."

"My dad bought it," I whisper, the words catching in my throat. Normally we just shop online, but he said that for the first day of middle school, we could spend the whole day shopping at the mall together and even get frozen yogurt. Grandma Colleen was there, too, since she lives with us now, but he didn't let her argue about how much money we were spending. The skirt wasn't even on sale. Not even close to on sale. At $59.50 it's the most expensive piece of clothing I own (except for my winter coat, but Dad says I'll wear that for years since it never gets too cold in Teravista, Texas, a suburb just north of Austin).

Dad picked out the top, a white T-shirt with "Fabulous" written in shimmering turquoise letters with these little tassels that hang beneath. "Because you *are* fabulous," he said. We tried on the whole outfit last Wednesday before he left for work in Chicago, and he took my first-day-of-school picture on the front porch even though it technically wasn't. We tried to have Grandma take one of me and Dad with his phone, but she kept getting it blurry or putting her finger in it, so we only have the one of me. Dad said the outfit was perfect.

"It's a great skirt, just not for school. You wouldn't wear a bikini to school, right? Same thing with short skirts. No time at Live Oak Middle School for any distractions."

I'm a distraction? Ms. Scott taps my shoulder, and I turn around. My cheeks flame with embarrassment.

"Take this note to the front office, and they'll give your dad a call." She scribbles on a small yellow notepad. "If he can't bring you a change of clothes, they'll find you something in the nurse's office to wear. No one gets suspended for dress code on the first day."

Suspended! I grab the note and rush to my desk, cramming my notebook and my perfect first-day-of-school mechanical pencil into my bag. I sneak along the edge of the classroom, hoping no one sees me, but of course they do. They're all staring at me and my distracting skirt. One boy turns and whispers to his friend, but mostly everyone's mouths just hang open in shock.

"Margie, what's going on?" Daniela whispers, but I can't open my mouth. I pull down on my skirt and race out the door.

chapter 2

I AM **NOT** MY DRESS.

"We've got extra extra small or extra extra large. What's your pick?"

Nurse Angela holds up two pairs of gym shorts that look like they've been in a locker for years. Are they even clean? She's wearing scrubs with teacups on them, and she smiles, the only comforting thing in her bare office. I waited for twenty minutes in one of the plastic chairs outside after an eighth-grade office aide dropped me off; Nurse Angela was giving a sixth grader his meds. I was hoping she'd forget I was waiting. She didn't.

Nurse Angela spreads the shorts out on her desk as if I'm supposed to judge between two prized dogs at the National Dog Show Grandma Colleen loves to watch at Thanksgiving. Both shorts will go down to my knees because they're that baggy-gym-shorts style—but the extra-extra-small pair looks much cleaner. The stripe down the side is still crisp white, and the Live Oak Middle School emblem hasn't started curling around the edges or been picked off by previous wearers. Still, there's no way I can fit into the extra extra small. But I don't know how I'll keep the extra extra large from falling down as I walk around school.

"So?" Nurse Angela asks as she gives the shorts a little shake. Their stale smell floats into my nostrils. Bleachy? I hope so. I take the extra-extra-large pair.

"Thattagirl! You can change in here."

She gestures toward a narrow door I thought was a closet, maybe is a closet. Please, oh, please may it have a little door that leads to Narnia or some other world so I don't have to come out wearing someone's stinky old gym shorts.

I open the door, and it's only a bathroom. There's a tiny window up in the corner, too high for me to reach, and no little escape hatch. I sit on the toilet seat lid with the shorts in my lap.

I don't want to cry. Not on my first day of middle school.

I cried every day the first month of kindergarten.

I cried every day the first week of sleepaway camp.

I don't want to cry on the first day of middle school.

But here I am using these old shorts as a tissue. They don't smell as bad up close as I thought they would.

"Get movin', little lady," Nurse Angela calls through the closed door. Then, softer, "No one's gonna care what you're wearing."

She knows nothing about middle school.

I change into the shorts, ignoring the mirror. In my backpack I find a hair tie to wrap around a corner of the waistband to keep them up, but then it gives me a weird tail. So I remove the hair tie and roll the waistband down three times instead, causing a doughnut effect around my hips. I walk back and forth between the sink and the toilet a few times, and if I push my hips forward or backward, the shorts don't slide as much. I'm not sure which looks sillier, the tail or the lump, but nothing can be worse than losing my pants in the hallway.

I finally look at myself in the mirror: my "Fabulous" shirt laughing at the disaster happening below. My curly hair's expanding in the humidity, and behind my blue glasses my eyes are ringed in red. I flip over the St. Joan of Arc pendant Dad bought for my birthday last year, noticing I've already chipped my turquoise nail polish.

Setting my glasses on the miniscule sink, I splash a bit of water on my face and dry it with some toilet paper since the paper towel machine is empty. For a moment I'm grateful Dad won't let me wear anything more than lip gloss so I don't have black streaks down my face like sobbing ladies in movies. I fold up my skirt—the perfect skirt—and stuff it in my backpack. I hear Grandma Colleen's voice in the back of my head. *You think you have it rough? When I was a child in Ireland, we had to walk two miles to school with only a hot potato in our pocket to keep us warm.*

Today, I would rather have the hot potato and the two-mile walk.

When I open the door, Nurse Angela is snacking from a bag of almonds. "You said your dad's in Chicago, but is there anyone else who could bring you a change of clothes?"

The tears catch in my throat, and I hold really still, no breathing, no blinking until the feeling goes away. Last night on the phone, Dad kept apologizing for missing my first day. That's why he let Grandma and me order Chinese takeout, but it doesn't change the fact that he's not here when I need him. It's only me and him (well, and now Grandma), since Mom died of breast cancer before I was two, so he tries to be around as much as he can. Up until a year ago he worked from home, so he was always hovering, practically smothering me with his desire to be a good dad. Then his company got bought by a firm in Chicago. Now he has an office in downtown Austin for weekdays and monthly trips to meet with his bosses in the Windy City. He's constantly missing my first somethings.

"No, I don't have anyone else I can call."

"You have your grandma listed as a contact. Can she bring you something?"

I shake my head, clutching my backpack closer to me. "She can't drive anymore. She has cataracts."

"Well, I guess you'll just have to sport a little Live Oak pride today."

I nod. I feel a lot of Live Oak shame today.

"You can head back to class now. Just let me write you a pass."

I put my backpack on the floor and stand at the desk as she fills out a yellow pass with the messiest handwriting I've ever seen. The blue squiggles can't possibly be words. The bell rings, and Nurse Angela looks at her watch. "Second period already?"

I missed all of first period. My first period of middle school. I won't see Daniela now until lunch, I think. I didn't get to check our schedules. We were supposed to do that in first period. My stomach clenches.

"Do you think I can stay here a little while? My stomach hurts."

Nurse Angela looks up at me like I'm a little

puppy left out in the rain. "That's not your stomach hurting; that's your pride."

She hands me the yellow pass, and I grab my backpack, brushing off the dust that's already clinging to the pink flamingo fabric. I yank my shorts up.

"Have a great first day!" Nurse Angela calls as I walk out the door.

She has got to be kidding.

As I walk down the crowded hallways, jostled by people running and laughing and loving their cute first-day outfits, I think of an alter ego, like a spy on a secret mission. If anyone asks, I won't be Margaret Colleen Kelly today. I'll be someone else. Someone lame. Someone who would wear rolled up gym shorts on the first day of school. And then tomorrow I can come to school with French braids or even a new hair color if Dad will let me, and no one will remember me as the girl with the baggy, stinky gym shorts lumped around her waist.

I stick close to the yellow lockers no kids use, watching the older girls pass by in faded skinny jeans and plaid shirts loosely hanging over tight tank tops. They don't bother to look at me, too busy trying to sneak a peek at their phones while they walk.

"Ahhhhh, dress coooooooode!" someone yells, and I turn to see a tall boy pointing at me, his mouth open in laughter as he tries to get his friend to turn and look. I start to walk faster, bumping into someone's shoulder. I notice a girl's phone pointed in my direction. Is she filming me? Please don't let her post this to Instagram! She flips her black hair over her shoulder and shoves the phone in her back pocket. Maybe it wasn't about me at all.

"Margie!" Daniela calls from somewhere in the crowd behind me. "Margie, wait!" It's only been a minute, and already my cover is blown. I'm instantly jealous when I'm reminded how perfect Daniela's first-day-of-school outfit is for her: cuffed black jeans and a short-sleeved blue button-up with little birds all over it, her thick dark hair in a massive braid down her back. She's been wanting to cut it short since last year, but her mom won't let her. Grandma Colleen would call Daniela a "tomboy," but no one says that anymore. Over the summer, Daniela finally stopped wearing exclusively summer camp T-shirts and one pair of light-wash blue jeans, but she still dislikes dresses and skirts. The only dress she ever wore was for her First Communion, and that's only because her mom made her. She's still figuring out her style, figuring out what (and who) she likes. Of course, Daniela's not wearing makeup—she would never ever ever—but she doesn't need it with her thick eyelashes and flawless brown skin. She's never even had a zit. I haven't, either, but any red spots will blare like sirens on my pale, freckled face.

"Get out of my way!" Daniela yells to some really tall boys who are playing keep-away with a bag of potato chips. "What happened, Margie? Where did you go? I saw you with Ms. Scott and..."

Daniela looks down at the gym shorts, her thick, black eyebrows raised. She touches my shoulder. "Did you get your...you know? I might have a jacket you could wrap around your waist."

"No," I say shrugging off her hand, even though it did feel nice. Daniela and I have been best friends ever since we ended up in the same second-grade class at Greenlawn Elementary and the same First

Communion group at Saint Mark's. She's the only person who can calm me down, because unlike me, she never panics. When we're getting crushed at summer league softball, she can still throw the perfect pitch. She got left in the museum bathroom on our fourth-grade field trip, and she didn't cry or start running after the bus. She just went to the front desk and had them call the school. She even knew the number. She stresses about her grades, and she's obsessed with Quiz Bowl, but for all other situations, she's like the perfect firefighter or paramedic.

Daniela leans in to whisper, "Did you have an accident?"

"No! Gross! I'm not a little kid!" We're blocking the hallway, so I pull her toward the lockers.

"Then what happened?"

"My skirt was out of dress code. Didn't you see Ms. Scott measuring me?"

"Yeah, but she made you change? On the first day? That's so harsh. Can your dad bring you some other clothes?"

"He's in Chicago again! He doesn't get back until tonight."

"Oh," she says, grabbing my hand. Daniela knows how much I hate having my dad gone all the time. "I'm so sorry. Your skirt wasn't even that short."

"Short enough to get me dress coded on my first day of school." Tonight I'll have to research any other violations in the student handbook Dad supposedly has. It's probably somewhere in the desk drawer where he crams all the bank notices and school flyers. Who knows what other social-life bombs are waiting for me?

"You better go to class," I tell her. "You'll be late."

"I'll walk you to yours; I don't want you to be alone."

Daniela wouldn't care if she was wearing dorky shorts on her first day. People always assume things about her anyway—that she's not as smart because she speaks Spanish, that she loves soccer because she's Mexican—so she doesn't care about anyone's opinions. Except for her parents. I wish I were that brave.

"I have a pass. Just go."

"Are you sure? I can come with you."

I shake my head, letting go of her hand. "I'll be okay."

I start walking toward the staircase that I think—hope—takes me to my math class.

"Don't forget to meet me outside the eighth-grade building after school," Daniela calls. "Quiz Bowl tryouts."

I freeze. This can't be happening. "It's not today. Not till Wednesday."

Daniela shakes her head. "They read an announcement in first period. It got moved to today. The teacher, Mr. Shao, has an appointment or something."

Daniela and I have been waiting for Quiz Bowl tryouts since the beginning of fifth grade. Our social studies and math teacher, Ms. Mackenzie, is a trivia champion, and we always did our own competition at the end of every unit. Daniela and I aced all the in-class competitions. Ms. Mackenzie called us the Queens of Quiz. Wednesday we were going to show up and shock everyone that sixth graders could be the best. Even though Daniela spent the summer with her abuela in Ojinaga, Mexico, we still texted or called almost every day so we could work through all the middle school question packets and even one of the high school sets. I had the perfect outfit (blue jean shorts, polka-dot top) picked out for Wednesday's tryout.

This can't be happening. I can't be the Quiz Bowl Queen when I'm dressed like a joker.

"Don't worry. It's going to be great," Daniela yells as the bell begins to ring. "Maybe you can change back into your real clothes before tryouts. See you at lunch!"

My gym shorts and I slink down the hallway, hoping a seat will be left in the back of every class.

chapter 3

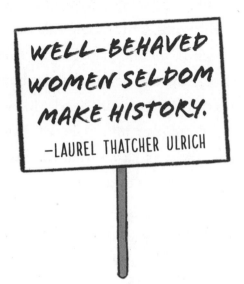

WELL-BEHAVED
WOMEN SELDOM
MAKE HISTORY.
—LAUREL THATCHER ULRICH

Quiz Bowl captains Marcus and Mikey hover over their friend Sean, who is setting out the buzzer system in Mr. Shao's freezing classroom. In front of them are two rectangular tables in face-off position. Together Marcus and Mikey stand like twin guardians of the Greek gods on Mount Olympus, ready to decide who's worthy and who's not. Black identical twins, the brothers share the same athletic arms bursting from their green Live Oak

Middle School polos, and the same haircuts—short on the sides with tight curls on top. Both have perfect smiles and the kind of eyes you could get lost in. Yes, they're that cute. Only Mikey's glasses set them apart. I've been in middle school all of eight hours, and already I know they're the popular boys. Nerds and athletes. Marcus has a girlfriend. Mikey has tons of people gushing over him at lunch. Everyone at school knows them and loves them and wants to be them. And they are the captains, the Kings of Quiz Bowl.

But Daniela and I are here, too. Hopefully, there's room for two sets of royalty.

We're the only sixth-grade girls in the room. Two of only three girls, when you count eighth grader Jamiya, but she doesn't talk to us. Probably because she's already on the team. Or because we're sixth graders. Maybe because I look like a dork since I wasn't allowed to change. Jamiya's wearing black high-rise jeans (in dress code), a T-shirt with pink hands making a peace sign (also dress code), and her natural hair pulled into a puff at the top of her head. Her fingers fly as she taps on her phone and occasionally makes fun of the boys. She's the team's social media manager, and I've read all her perfect Instagram posts from last season. She's funny and smart and a great photographer, somehow making buzzer systems and question packets look cool. She clearly doesn't mind that she's one of the few girls here.

Daniela and I wait along the wall, leaning against posters of American history that were probably printed before I was born and faded school projects that have been hanging for years. Four boys from sixth grade and two from seventh are also here to try out.

"I wasn't expecting it to be all boys, but at least it's not all white kids," Daniela whispers.

I scan the room, noticing that the group is more diverse than I saw on last year's Instagram posts. Maybe the new coach, Mr. Shao, had something to do with it. We watch Sean rush around, running a hand through his unruly red curls as he untangles the buzzer system. Any moment we'll be moving on to round two of the tryouts, and I'm sure everyone is doing exactly what I am: trying to churn up some confidence by reviewing all the facts I learned this summer.

For round one, we took a twenty-five-question multiple-choice test. The seventh and eighth graders already on the team joked around, sitting on top of the desks and rocking them back and forth as they talked about some app I've never heard of. They should have been quiet while we were testing, but it didn't matter. I only missed three questions. I think.

"You better get movin' since you've only got twenty minutes left," Mr. Shao calls from across the room. His desk is a mess: papers piled as high as his computer screen and an old banana peel on top of one stack. You'd think that as the Quiz Bowl adviser, he would be one of those adults who wished they were back in middle school, so they could still be on the debate team or standing on the stage at nationals answering the final question, but Mr. Shao doesn't seem to care about Quiz Bowl. He introduced himself when we got here, but then went straight to his desk where he's been ever since. He seems more like a babysitter than a coach.

Finally, Sean untangles the last cord and nods to

the Kings. Marcus looks down at the stack of tests on Mr. Shao's podium.

"We're doing five to a team instead of the normal four so we can get through everyone. Make a name tag when you sit down, and be sure we can read it. Mikey, you lead this team..." He pauses to assess the group. "Boy in the meme shirt, seventh graders, and girl with the braid. Take a seat at Table One."

I tap Daniela's hand, and she squeezes mine back. "Queens of Quiz," she whispers, and I smile, knowing we got this. Hoping we do. She waves as she picks up her backpack and sits at Table One.

"Jamiya, you'll be the moderator. I'll take notes. Elman, you lead the other team. Dress Code Girl"— my cheeks flame as the older kids snicker; thankfully the sixth graders are too worried about their performance to comment—"the rest of you, Table Two. Obviously."

We all move to the table, but no one takes a seat. Who sits where? Of course, Elman takes the middle seat as temporary captain, but the three other sixth-grade boys and I just hover, not knowing where to sit.

"You," Marcus says, pointing to a boy in a black

hoodie I recognize from visual media. "Next to Elman. You in the Cowboys jersey, next to him. You two can sit at the other end."

I look over at the tiny blond boy beside me, his enormous backpack folding him over like a turtle. He pauses, and I rush to take the seat next to the captain. I also grab the blue marker for my name tag before someone else can snatch it.

Once we're all seated, Marcus explains the rules for today's tryouts: Jamiya will read as many questions as she can before 5:15 PM, when after-school clubs end. Like normal Quiz Bowl, there will be toss-up questions that we answer by ourselves, and if we get those correct, bonus questions where we confer as a team. Normally, if we answer a toss-up question before the power mark, we get fifteen points. Then, ten points after that and ten points for all bonus questions. But no one is keeping score today; it doesn't matter who wins. Instead, Marcus will be taking notes on the questions we individually answer right. And the ones we answer wrong. "Don't be wrong," he says with a grin. I take a deep breath, wishing my confidence wasn't rolled up in my backpack with my perfect first-day skirt.

Marcus steps between the two tables, grabs a clipboard from the podium, and takes a dramatically long time to stare us down. Then he breaks into an enormous smile: "Let's quiz."

Jamiya's practiced voice reads out the first question: "This emperor became infamous—"

Mikey slams on his buzzer, the center light glowing red. "Nero."

"Are you sure?" Marcus asks. "You think there's only one infamous emperor in history?" He's the only one allowed to question Mikey. Only a king can challenge a king.

"I wouldn't have said 'Nero' if I wasn't sure."

Marcus turns to Jamiya for confirmation. "Correct. Nero. Fifteen points," she says.

Marcus frowns and Mikey slaps his hand on the table, hooting with laughter. "These questions are from last year's national championship. I memorized them all."

The seventh and eighth graders already on the

team start murmuring, and Mikey stops them with a hand. "Don't worry. I won't answer any more."

Jamiya playfully hits his shoulder before reading more questions. José on Daniela's team incorrectly answers a toss-up about U-boats, but no one on our team knows it either and the question goes dead. Then, we have to work out a computation on the back of old history worksheets. I hit my buzzer but get beaten by Daniela. I'm okay with that. Mostly. With every question, Mikey taps his hand on the table within seconds of Jamiya's first words, a signal to us all that he knows more than we ever could. Thankfully, I answer a toss-up about Dobby from Harry Potter, but Xavier beside me gets the next one about the constellation Orion.

"You've got five minutes, and those buzzers better be put away," Mr. Shao calls from his desk, a napkin tucked into his shirt as he eats a burrito I didn't hear him microwave.

I need more time! I only answered one right!

"Go ahead and do their bonus questions," Marcus instructs Jamiya. "And then we'll stop."

"This is a bonus question for Team Two," Jamiya

says, and we all lean forward, even though our captain will have to make our final answer. "To describe the pilgrims in his narrative collection of poems, this author employs physiognomy to..." She slows over the pronunciation, which gives me just enough time to realize I 100 percent know this answer. I don't bother to listen to the rest; I can see Dad with his copy of *The Canterbury Tales* by Geoffrey Chaucer, the one he got in college when he was still an English major. He has a really old copy he got from one of his professors, and when I was little, I thought it was a hundred years old because of its faded green fabric and pressed letters, but really it was just from the seventies.

"I know this!" I whisper, and Elman puts up a hand to shush me so he can finish listening. We only have five seconds after the question is read to answer.

"Is it Shakespeare?" Xavier whispers.

Elman shakes his head. "I don't think so."

"It's Geoffrey Chaucer!" I say, almost yelling because I'm so excited. "I one hundred percent know this. My dad has—"

"William Wordsworth!" Elman says, smiling at

his wrong answer. Then he pauses. "Maybe it was Shakespeare."

"No, it's not!" I argue, and all the boys look at me. Marcus leans in, too.

"Are you sure?" asks Eliot, his face shadowed by his hoodie, and I sigh.

"Yes."

"Team, we need an answer," Jamiya says, and Elman looks at me. I give him a thumbs-up because yes, I for sure, cross-my-heart-and-hope-to-die know this.

"William Shakespeare," Elman says, and I can't stop the "No!" from escaping.

"Incorrect," Jamiya says, and the boys at Table One start howling, making jokes about Elman as he tries to recover.

"Okay, folks, it's almost five o'clock. Start packing up!" Mr. Shao shouts from his desk, leaning over to flick the lights on and off.

"Decent work," Marcus says, still clutching his clipboard. "We'll post the new team roster tomorrow."

As we pack up, I wait for Elman to apologize and say I was right, but the older kids leave the room laughing and joking and don't even bother to show us sixth graders out.

Daniela comes over to my table and tugs one of my curls. "You knew that one!"

"I know."

"This has not been your day," she says, pulling out a bag of Skittles and offering me a few.

Tomorrow has to be better. Maybe I can just pretend my second day of middle school is my first and forget this day ever happened.

chapter 4

I'M SORRY, DID MY KNEES DISTRACT YOU FROM READING THIS POSTER?

"Next," Dad calls out from the living room where he and Grandma Colleen are waiting like judges on a TV talent show.

"Hold on!" I yell from my bedroom as I struggle with the button on an old denim skirt. It doesn't really fit anymore, but as soon as Dad got in from Chicago, he dug out the student handbook and said I needed to try on all my skirts and shorts. I knew I grew over the summer, but who would have thought three-quarters of an inch could do so much damage to my wardrobe?

I wasn't going to tell Dad anything—not about the skirt, not about Quiz Bowl tryouts—but Nurse Angela left him a voice mail this morning. He thinks the whole dress code thing is ridiculous—draconian middle school rules—but that's only because I didn't tell him about Ms. Scott measuring me in front of the class. Or the humiliating shorts. It's all too embarrassing to talk about, even with Dad.

After the Quiz Bowl tryout, I changed back into my skirt in the eighth-grade bathroom and shoved the stinky, parachute gym shorts into the bottom of my backpack. I'm supposed to wash and return them, but Grandma Colleen does all the laundry, and I don't want her asking questions. She used to work at a hotel in Houston, so she inspects all our clothes like a detective looking for evidence. Apparently when Dad was young, she would bring home clothes from the lost and found for him and his brother, Jeremy. She'd wash them in superhot water and then present them as new, but Dad was afraid every time he wore them, just waiting for some kid to point and say, "Hey! That's my jacket!" I could wash the shorts myself, but Grandma's room is right next to the washer and dryer. I'll probably just throw them away, since there's no way the school cares about those dingy, old gym shorts.

So Dad knows the skirt was too short, but he thinks I just got a reminder and then spent the day skipping through middle school like the perfect first-day kid in her perfect first-day skirt. When he texted me at lunch to see how things were going, I sent a smiley face emoji. Since I'm an only child, he talks to me as a real human being and not "just a kid": he doesn't pry into my business unless I'm being suspicious. Or crying. He always asks a bajillion questions when I'm crying.

Dad wonders why the school spends time on such trivial things as measuring clothes when American students are thirtieth in the world in math and refugees are still risking their lives in inflatable boats. He believes in girl power and even took me to the Women's March last year, but that didn't stop him from beginning his own measuring mission to confirm my clothes were no more than four inches above the knee. Dad is willing to follow rules even if he doesn't like them.

"Margie, hurry up, we still need to eat dinner, and it's getting late!"

I sigh, leaving the button only halfway through the buttonhole, and trudge to the living room. Dad and Grandma Colleen sit on the edge of the couch, our old burgundy and navy pillows slouched behind them. Grandma is sipping tea from one of the fancy teacups she brought with her when she moved in last year after her cataract surgery.

I didn't think she'd stay forever. Grandma certainly didn't. She's always been independent, ever since she flew over from Skibbereen, County Cork, Ireland, when she was nineteen to live with cousins in New Jersey. She raised Dad and Uncle Jeremy by herself in Houston after Grandpa Teddy died of a heart attack when Dad was in middle school. Since I've known her, she's loved living by herself with her little potted plants in old coffee cans that covered every counter in her house and her stacks of celebrity magazines that she scoured while sitting on the porch. She loved her scrappy little dog, Milton. She had to give him to her neighbor since Dad is allergic.

After she had complications from the first surgery and lost some sight in her right eye, Dad decided she had better move in with us. Uncle Jeremy lives in a New York City studio, so there was no way she could live with him. It took Dad two weeks to empty her house and move all her rose teacups and picture frames and old copies of *People* and *Entertainment Weekly* into what used to be his office. Jeremy didn't even come down to help her move. He was too busy with work. Dad said he was too busy with Jeremy. Now Grandma is here with us, sipping tea, gushing about the Kennedys as if they're still famous, and criticizing practically everything I do. All. Day. Long.

I try not to roll my eyes since it's disrespectful, but Grandma isn't making this whole thing any easier. She hasn't taken a single fashion tip from any of the celebrities she reads about. Her idea of fashionable is a perfectly pressed white blouse with a pale-green sweater draped over her shoulders. She's the opposite of Daniela's abuela, who is all about bright patterns and big sunglasses. Sometimes people confuse her for Daniela's mom. People sometimes think my grandma is a nun.

Dad smiles like a goofball when he sees me. He looks me over, the ruler in his freckled hand. As he stares at my curly hair, my pointy nose speckled with a few freckles, the eyebrows I would pluck if it didn't hurt so bad, and of course the skirt, he gets that smile when he's thinking about Mom. He doesn't say it so often that it means nothing, but some days he'll see me and get that smile and say, "You look just like your mom."

Honestly, I look more like Dad. He's short, not much taller than I am, with cropped brown hair that's thinning at the top and lots of freckles covering his thick arms and legs. We both wear glasses, but his are nerdy black frames while mine are more of a subtle blue. We look Irish, as Grandma tells me all the time—blue eyes, sunburn-ready skin, and tawny brown hair—so I don't know what he sees of Mom in me. She had hazel eyes and hair that went gray in her twenties, so she always dyed it, usually shades of red. She was really tall—almost six feet—and could rest her chin on Dad's head. He said he hated and loved when she did that. I often stare at the pictures of her on my dresser, trying to find ways we're similar, comparing our eyebrows, the way our eyes crinkle when we smile. I don't have any real memories of her, but I miss her just the same. It's not missing exactly, since I have no idea what it would be like to have a mom, but there's a hole, a space inside me that remains unfilled.

Sometimes Dad reminds me of other things I got from her: my habit of forgetting cups of water around the house, my hatred of anything coconut flavored, my tireless ability to argue. And he says we both have hearts too big for our bodies. Mom was a social worker who helped homeless clients find jobs and housing. She brought communion to church members who couldn't come to mass and was constantly attending rallies in Austin on the state capitol steps. I do volunteer at the nursing home with Junior Catholic Daughters and cry whenever I see abandoned animals, but I don't think my heart is as big as hers. Maybe when I get my growth spurt.

"This one looks like it's going to miss the mark," Dad says, as he holds out the ruler he found in the kitchen junk drawer. "But I love this skirt on you. I remember when we bought it."

"Doesn't matter. Just measure it," I say. I turn around, and Dad measures the back of the skirt.

"As I suspected, Watson, this skirt is one half inch shorter than the requirement." His fake British accent doesn't make this any more fun.

"I can just slide it down a little bit." When I do that, it almost reaches the top of my kneecaps. "But it doesn't really fit anymore anyway. Look."

I show him the button.

"I can fix that," Grandma says, taking another sip of her tea and readjusting her dentures with her tongue. So. Gross. Apparently when you get old, you have to move your teeth around sometimes.

"Nope. It's not in compliance. Put it in the weekend pile if you want Grandma to adjust the button." Dad gestures to the three piles of clothes: one for school, one for weekends and vacations, and one for Goodwill. Only three skirts and one pair of shorts have survived to be worn in the halls of Live Oak Middle School.

"Such a waste," Grandma grumbles. "Perfectly

good clothes. We should give some to that little friend of yours."

"Daniela? No way. She doesn't wear skirts."

I drop the skirt on the giveaway pile, wishing it a fond farewell before it heads off to its new life at Goodwill. Even if Grandma adjusts the button, it will be too tight soon anyway.

Dad yawns, covering his mouth with his hand before taking off his glasses and rubbing his eyes. "We need to wrap this up, kiddo, so we can eat before nine. Is this it?"

I nod, slumping onto the chair across from them.

"Seems like a lot of clothes for a little girl," Grandma says.

"Wait. Go put on the offending skirt. I want to measure it for myself," Dad says, and I shake my head. "Come on. It'll be the last one. I have to see it."

"No! You know it's too short already."

"You told me it was, but I haven't seen it. And I really liked that skirt. We picked it out together, our father-daughter bonding."

Heat rushes to my eyes as I think about our day at the mall, the first time in weeks we got to spend the whole day together. Standing in front of the mirror at the store, I felt invincible. I felt brave.

"It's too short," I say, sinking into the chair's oversized cushions.

"Go get it," he says, his voice getting deeper.

"No."

Dad frowns. "You've now said no three times in two minutes. I get that you're upset, Marge, but I want to measure it myself. Maybe the school was wrong."

"Fine!" I huff and storm out over Grandma's grumbling about me respecting my father. Despite what she thinks, I don't need another parent. I've been doing fine with just one.

In my room, I grab the skirt off my laundry pile. It's wrinkled from having been rolled up in my backpack all day. I lay it out on my blue floral comforter, sliding my hands across the three tiers. The fabric is so soft, almost like pajamas. I pull it on, and it still looks great with my "Fabulous" T-shirt. This morning in front of the mirror, I felt so ready in this outfit, as if the skirt was the final touch in all our preparations for middle school. Dad and I have picked first-day-of-school outfits every year since pre-K, but this year it mattered. Everyone tells you how horrible middle school is: lonely lunches, the drama, hours of homework. This skirt was going to keep me from having the middle school nightmares everyone else experienced. But it doesn't feel perfect anymore. I don't feel perfect.

Dad beams when I walk back into the living room. "That is a killer first-day outfit."

Even Grandma nods. "It's classy. Like Meryl Streep."

I don't say anything as I turn around so he can measure. For the tenth time today, the ruler lies against my skin. My throat tightens as I remember standing behind Ms. Scott's desk, feeling the eyes of all my classmates on me. I think about the gym shorts and the stares and Marcus calling me "Dress Code Girl" and the way my first day of sixth grade could have gone. Should have gone.

"Yikes, this one is an inch and a half too short. It didn't look that short when we bought it. I guess it was a couple of weeks ago...."

I start to sniffle, a teardrop falling onto my bare feet.

"Oh, honey, what's wrong?" Dad says, turning me toward him. "You can wear this one at home, and we'll get new skirts for school. I've got to get some work done this weekend, but you can go with your grandma."

Shopping with her would be worse than wearing those gym shorts. I'll end up looking like a ninety-year-old lady from one of her rosary prayer groups.

"I don't want to talk about it anymore," I whisper, already pulling away. I scoop up the piles of skirts and shorts, ready to stuff them all in the trash. For now, I'll throw them in my closet, so I won't see them and be reminded of the worst first day of school ever.

chapter 5

NOT A
DISTRACTION.

The next day, I am back in Ms. Scott's class, this time in a pair of cropped jeans. I didn't have the energy to risk shorts or a skirt today, even though they've all been measured. When I walked in, Ms. Scott looked at my pants, winked, and gave me a thumbs-up. I was just glad she didn't say anything as I slunk to my desk. Thankfully, the girl between Daniela and me is absent so we can talk.

"Do you think we both made the team?" Daniela

whispers as she writes her warm-up. "I wish they would have told us how many new kids they're taking."

"I know," I whisper back, no longer confident enough to say, "We definitely made the team!" I thought yesterday was *definitely* going to be amazing, and it *definitely* wasn't. Daniela has to make the team; she didn't take one day off from studying—unlike me, who spent a few days watching Netflix and swimming at the pool. I don't know what I'll do if she makes the team and I don't. I didn't imagine middle school without us being the Queens of Quiz.

"We have to go see the posting together. Right after school," Daniela says, and I nod as I put a period on my last sentence. A timer buzzes, and Ms. Scott calls Dylan, a boy from our fifth-grade class, to the front of the room. Everyone but Daniela had a crush on Dylan at some point in fourth or fifth grade. He was the leader of all sports games at recess. He was bigger than everybody in fifth grade except Ashley M., but she had really pale skin and could never be in the sun more than a few minutes, so she never participated. He has this swoopy brown hair that sometimes falls in his eyes, and he can run so fast. That's why I liked him for the little bit of time I did. My legs are strong but not speedy, and there was something about watching him sprint across the playground with his flowing hair that just got to me.

Dylan walks to the front of the classroom, and Ms. Scott hands him a ruler to point to the goal for the day. I didn't think we'd have to do choral reading like this in sixth grade, but he points to "Students" and we all begin reading "Students will review the literary characteristics of plot." Before we get to the end, I see it.

Dylan's blue plaid shorts are too short.

Suddenly I'm panicked for him. There's no way he'll make it back to his desk before Ms. Scott notices the enormous gap between the end of his shorts and his kneecaps. Ms. Scott talks about homework, and Dylan smiles at the class, winking at one of his friends and swinging the ruler back and forth. He's like a baby antelope in one of those National Geographic shows Dad watches with me. He doesn't know the lion is lurking. Ms. Scott moves on to the agenda, and my heartbeat races as Dylan's ruler taps each item. I'm not friends with Dylan, and I don't have a crush on him anymore, but I wouldn't wish the ruler on anyone.

"Look," I whisper to Daniela.

"What?" she asks, and Ms. Scott shoots us one of those teacher looks: wide eyes and raised eyebrows, a silent "shhh."

I can't bear the weight of watching this alone. But how can I tell Daniela without getting in trouble? Again. I flip my notebook to the back and write, "Dylan's shorts" with an arrow pointing to where he's still oblivious at the board. He has mere seconds before his job is done and Ms. Scott calls him over to the desk of doom.

Daniela looks down at my notebook, then at me, her face all scrunched up in confusion. I point to the shorts and make my eyes really big. She looks down at the words and then up at him, and then her head snaps back to me, her face registering understanding.

"Too short!!!!" she writes in her own notebook, and I nod.

Together we wait.

"Thank you, Dylan, you may take a seat," Ms. Scott finally says, and he walks back to his desk. I wonder which gym shorts he'll wear since the extra-extra-large pair is still in my bedroom. Were there more options, and Nurse Angela just showed me two? People won't be crushing on Dylan when he's wearing those dorky shorts, but maybe his parents can bring him something else to wear. I remember his mom bringing kale cupcakes to school a lot, even when it wasn't his birthday.

Dylan takes his seat next to a kid from a different elementary. Ms. Scott hands out short stories, explaining the assignment for the day, but I'm hardly listening as I wait for her to get to Dylan. She'll put her hand on his shoulder—I can feel it on mine now. "Come see me at my desk," she'll say with a sad face, feeling sympathy for this poor, foolish boy, and he won't know what's happening. Well, maybe he'll remember me from yesterday, but probably not or he would not have risked those shorts.

Daniela and I stare as Ms. Scott reaches his desk. She lays down the short stories and pauses. Here it is. The hand should be reaching...and she's walking away. Daniela looks at me and I shrug. Maybe she'll wait until we're working?

She does nothing. I watch her for the entire forty-eight minutes of class, waiting, waiting, for the moment, but she never pulls Dylan over to her desk. She never asks him about the handbook. She never places the ruler on the back of his legs. Dylan and his blue plaid shorts are safe. He is not a distraction.

That is so unfair!

"Fourteen," I tell Daniela when we get to lunch. I point to the columns I've made in the back of my notebook. "Fourteen boys wearing shorts way above their knees. Two girls with questionable skirts and five girls wearing the ugly gym shorts. Do you know how many boys were wearing them?"

Daniela looks at me over her taco salad. "One?"

"Zero!" I shout, loud enough that the nearby assistant principal points up at the stoplight in the front of the room indicating our volume should be yellow, for our neighbor only.

"Really? None?" Daniela argues. "Maybe you

just missed them. Or they're in the eighth-grade building."

I take a bite of my egg salad, choking it down because I'm so mad. (I actually love Grandma's egg salad.) Daniela always has to play the lawyer opposing my case, but I don't want to debate. I want to be outraged.

"I didn't think this sort of sexist stuff would happen in middle school. No one cared what we wore in elementary. And remember how Ms. Mackenzie never let us split into boy and girl groups? Don't they know about women's rights here? It's not fair. I started counting after third period, in class and in the hallway, and the evidence speaks for itself. Besides, look," I say, gesturing toward the full cafeteria. "Let's count here."

"Can we do this tomorrow?" Daniela says, looking down at a book on airplanes. "I need to prep a new area for Quiz Bowl. If we make the team, we're really going to have to prove ourselves, especially as sixth graders."

"Fine, you prep. I'll count."

I scan the crowd, focusing on the lines of kids

pressed against the wall, waiting to fill their trays with today's hot lunch: taco salad and a cup full of strawberries. An even mix of boys and girls wait in line, though they're all clumped together by friend groups, kids not even facing the right direction as they talk. I start with the boys since they're the ones getting off scot-free in this whole situation. Jeans, jeans, black gym shorts, really big gym shorts, skinny jeans, jeans showing some boxers.

"Look! Right there!" I shout, and Daniela chokes on her milk.

"What? Who?"

"That boy by the 'Be an Upstander not a Bystander' poster. In the bright-blue polo. His shorts are way too short." We stare down the sixth grader I don't recognize who is wearing khaki shorts as if he's going on safari. They're actually not that different from the cargo shorts Daniela is wearing, but there are definitely...five...six...too many inches of brown skin between his shorts and his kneecaps.

"But he is wearing tall socks," Daniela says, and I scoff.

"So? It's not about how much leg is covered. And

watch. He's going to walk right by that assistant principal in three...two...one..."

Again, we wait. And then the assistant principal gives him a high five. A high five! Are you kidding me?

"That is so unfair," Daniela says, sighing as she finishes her last bite of taco salad. She writes down a fact in her notebook.

"No wonder we don't have a woman president."

I stuff down the last of my egg salad. "Life isn't fair," Dad would tell me.

Life isn't fair...yet.

chapter 6

FIGHT
LIKE A
GIRL.

After school, a crowd of students has gathered outside Mr. Shao's door. It's all the same faces as yesterday, all the same *boys*, and they're lunging over one another like obsessed fans at a concert.

"Enough! Chill!" Marcus yells as he leaps over the stair railing behind Daniela and me. We both jump back and quickly follow him. "One at a time."

The huddle breaks like the universe expanding after the Big Bang. Marcus stands in front of the team roster hanging beside the door. Sean meanders over, snacking on an apple. They're clearly not freaking out like the rest of us.

"You first!" Marcus calls, pointing at José, who is again wearing a meme T-shirt, this time with Pikachu looking shocked. He's now in my third-period science class. José lifts his chin, pulling down on the straps of his backpack before taking a step toward Marcus. He doesn't reach Marcus's chin. They stare at each other for a minute, all of us waiting. Do we have to battle him to see it? Give him a bribe?

Apparently not, because Marcus steps aside. José scans the list, his finger running down the names. "Yes!" he cries, fist flying into the air. Marcus nods and gives him a fist bump before Sean opens the door to the classroom.

"You next," Marcus says, pointing at Daniela. She squeezes my hand before quickly doing the sign of the cross, pressing her thumb to her lips as she walks toward Marcus. She must have been praying the same prayer as me: please, Lord, may my name be on that list. My stomach hurts as I watch her finger slide down the paper. For a second, I hope she doesn't make the team if that means I do. I want us both to get it, of course I do, but if it can only be one girl, I hope it's me.

Come on, Daniela. She spins around. A smile. *Yes!*

She mouths, "I'll see you inside," and heads into the classroom. The sinking feeling in my gut doesn't go away as the next four boys are called. The two seventh graders make it through the door. Two sixth graders slink back down the hallway and up the stairs into the land of average knowledge.

Finally, Marcus's finger points at me. But also at the tiny blond boy beside me, Xavier. Is he doing this because we're the final two? Now he wants to speed up the process?

Xavier and I step toward the paper together as if our legs are tied for a three-legged race. Marcus crosses his arms over his chest and leans against the wall as we strain to read the tiny print. Kelly is never at the top of a list, so I start at the middle. It's not there. Xavier is scanning, too, his finger sliding up and down the list of names.

Then Marcus points to the bottom of the page.

Margie Kelly. Xavier Brooks. *Runoff.*

We both turn toward Marcus.

He smirks. "Looks like we're going to have a battle."

He puts a hand on Xavier's shoulder and moves us both through the door.

The buzzer box slips in my sweaty hands as Marcus paces back and forth between our desks. Across from me, Xavier looks like he's ready to slide out of his seat onto the floor. His face is so pale, he's almost translucent.

"It's a showdown. Best two out of three," Mikey says, hopping up to sit on the materials table at the front of the room. A stack of books cascade to the floor, but no one bothers to pick them up. Apparently Mr. Shao's at a staff meeting and won't be here to supervise. The room feels packed, even though there are only thirteen of us in this huge classroom. The rest of the Quiz Bowl team hovers around the sides of the desks, the newbies huddled in the corner as if they're afraid they might lose their spot and soon be sitting with us two. Daniela stands behind me, one hand on my chair.

"You got this," she whispers, and I close my eyes, taking a deep breath.

I don't know if I got this.

"I'll be the moderator," Marcus says. "If you're disqualified, you're done. No second chances."

Third chances, really, but I don't dare correct him.

"Ready?" he asks, a smile spreading across his face. Sean, who's been standing by the door, tosses his apple core in the trash with a clang.

"Let's go!"

"Question one," Marcus reads from a set of note cards he pulled from his hoodie pocket. "Occupying 3.16 percent of the night sky, this largest of the eighty-eight constellations contains three Messier objects—"

Bam! Xavier presses his buzzer, his red light burning in my eyes. "Hydra."

"That's correct. First point goes to Xavier."

Daniela pats my shoulder. "Don't worry. You know you're working on astronomy."

I clench my teeth, trying to shake it off. But sneaking into my head is the worry that I'd never even heard the term "Messier objects" before today. Maybe I'm not ready for middle school Quiz Bowl.

"Question two," Marcus reads, and I close my eyes to help myself focus, not worried if I look stupid. "In one play by this Pulitzer Prize–winning playwright, salesman Willy Loman fades into a series of daydreams in which he reimagines events from his past—"

I know this! I hit my buzzer, feeling confident as the red light in front of me blinks. "Arthur Miller."

Thank you, Dad, for dragging me to summer theater every year since I was born.

"Looks like we got ourselves a tie. Whoever answers the next question correctly, welcome to Quiz Bowl."

Mikey hops off the table, sending more books to the ground. He takes a step toward me. "Think you can handle it?"

Is that a real question? Does he want me to answer? "Ye—yes."

Elman leans over to give Xavier a high five. "Good luck, dude."

I get nothing. Looking around the room, the boys

are all grouped together, whispering and talking, leaving Daniela and Jamiya standing together behind me. Daniela whispers, "You can do this!"

Marcus shuffles through the note cards, smiling at some, wrinkling his nose at others. He finally picks one.

"Let me see!" Sean calls from across the room.

"Nah, you gotta wait like everyone else."

"Whatever," Sean says, sitting back in Mr. Shao's rolling chair. I don't know what Mr. Shao will say if he walks in and sees we've taken over his classroom like this.

Marcus stops between our desks, his body at attention like a LEGO man with his legs snapped to the floor. He whips the card in front of his face. "First orchestrating a nonviolent movement to achieve legal equality for African Americans, this man later shifted his focus to economic justice, organizing the Poor People's Campaign with the Southern Christian Leadership Conference shortly before his death."

My finger slams on the buzzer, but it's Xavier's red light that glows. Xavier pumps his fist before lifting his chin proudly. "Martin Luther King."

The room erupts into applause, all the boys coming to pat him on the back.

"Wait! That's not right!" I shout, standing up from my seat.

"Don't be a poor sport," Mikey yells from his throne.

"I'm not! But you can't accept 'Martin Luther King' without the 'Junior.' I know from fifth-grade—"

"It's not fifth grade anymore," someone says. My throat tightens.

"But that's the rules! He can say 'MLK,' but otherwise he has to say 'Junior.'" I remember watching the Texas Middle School Championship last year with Daniela when the Houston team almost lost the final by answering without the "Junior."

"She's right!" Jamiya says, her voice silencing everyone.

Marcus holds up his hand. "Your stupid cheering didn't allow me to say, 'Add more.'"

Daniela squeezes my shoulder. It's not over yet. Xavier's eyes flick between me and Marcus. Someone ruffles his blond hair.

"We'll do one last question," Marcus says, flipping through the stack. "And y'all need to shush!"

It's so quiet I can hear the rustle of the cards as he shuffles. Everyone has settled closer to our chairs, so close that I can smell their body spray. Finally, Marcus lifts up a card.

"In addition to helping identify the age of the universe, the Hubble Space Telescope provided evidence that galaxies may harbor—"

"Not astronomy," Daniela whispers, her hand slipping off my shoulder. My stomach drops. *Please not astronomy.* I glance at Xavier.

"—these supermassive structures—"

Boom! Xavier smacks the buzzer so hard he sends the box sailing over the edge of the table, yanking the other buzzer boxes down with it.

"Black holes!" he shouts, and the room waits, not wanting to disrupt like last time. I don't know if he's right or not.

Marcus smiles. "Welcome to the team, man!"

All the boys jump out of their seats, tackling Xavier as if he just ran the final touchdown to win the Super Bowl. Daniela wraps her arms around me, but no one else bothers to even tell me "Nice match." They don't notice as I slide out of my chair and head for my backpack at the back of the room. Daniela and Jamiya follow me, and I try to shake the stinging from my eyes, at least until I'm out of this personal black hole.

"You got robbed!" Daniela says. "You had him on Martin Luther King Jr. We know it has to have the 'Junior.'"

"I know."

"You still did really well," she says, putting her hand on my back while I zip and unzip my backpack, pretending to pack up.

"Would've been nice to have more girls on the team," Jamiya adds. "But at least it's not just me anymore."

"I'm gonna go," I say, knowing there's no reason for me to stay. The boys are still slapping Xavier on the back and showing each other things on their phones, so no one will notice me leave.

"Are you going to be okay? Will you take the late bus?"

"Yeah, I can go wait in the library."

"Definitely try out next year," Jamiya says before turning to the boys. "Y'all settle down so I can get a picture of the new team for Instagram."

My heart squeezes as I think about seeing their smiling faces tonight. I started following the team's Instagram this summer, hoping it would be me standing behind the buzzers. I grab my backpack.

"Hey, Dress Code," Marcus calls, walking toward me. "We need an alternate. You want it?"

Backup? To these boys? To a kid who didn't even know to add the "Junior"?

"I need to think about it."

Marcus shrugs. "That's fine, but let me know soon. And if you take it, you better learn your astronomy."

Tears burn the back of my throat.

"Got it," I say as I turn and run out the door, not stopping when Daniela calls my name.

chapter 7

When I get home, Grandma is at the kitchen table, completing the crossword in the back of her *People* magazine. I take off my shoes, dropping my backpack at the door.

"How are you doing?" I ask as she scribbles an all-caps "Tom" into the boxes with her favorite blue pen. She flips back to a page of women on the red carpet, scanning the captions with her finger.

"Almost finished."

"Wouldn't I look great in this one?" I ask, pointing to a bright-blue dress with a deep V-neckline that goes almost to the actress's belly button.

Grandma looks at me with horror. "Margaret!"

"Kidding!"

"You sit here and tell me what you learned at school," Grandma says, putting her pen down as a page marker. "I'll get you some tea."

What did I learn at school? Well, different rules apply to boys and girls, the Quiz Bowl Kings are really dictators who need to be overthrown, and things can only get worse.

"We learned proportions in math and the parts of a story in English." Grandma always wants details since she didn't finish high school. Her nightstand is covered with famous biographies and a few conspiracy theory books Dad says are fine since she's old and can't get on the internet. "But I'm going to call my friend in my room, Grandma."

She sighs. "Why does a young girl need her own phone?"

She says that every time she sees my phone, ever since I got it for my birthday this summer. It's not like I have complete freedom with it: Dad put on some parental controls to track my usage, and I have to charge it in the kitchen starting at 9:00 PM so I don't stay awake all night checking Instagram. Dad tried to explain to Grandma his reasons for getting me a phone—he's gone for work a lot now; most kids my age have a cell phone—but she didn't care. He stopped trying to explain. I never tried.

In my room, I change into my softest blue pajama pants and an old T-shirt from the Catholic summer camp I went to a few years ago, and flop onto the bed. For a few minutes, I just stare at the glow-in-the-dark stars on my ceiling and wonder how everything went so wrong. Then I grab my phone and call Daniela.

"¿Bueno?" Daniela's dad answers. I always have to call her mom or her dad's cell phone because Daniela doesn't have one. Her mom teaches at the dual language elementary school we went to, and she thinks technology is ruining kids' imaginations.

"Hi, Mr. Jaimes. It's Margie."

"Oh, hi, Margie. Just a minute. I'll get Daniela."

He goes to find her, and I listen to his footsteps,

picturing the house I know as well as my own: modern, white walls with lots of art and multicolored woven rugs; the red couch where we watch movies; the bright decorative pillows we once used in an epic pillow fight; sunny picture frames surrounding smiling faces (some including me).

"Hola, Margarita," Daniela's mom says over the sizzle of something on the stove. "Daniela casi termina en la ducha."

"Está bien," I say, even though I don't catch the rest. Daniela's mom always speaks to me in Spanish because I was in the dual language program, but I still have a hard time understanding some words. Or really long conversations. My brain gets tired trying to keep up. In the background, Daniela's baby brother, Miguel, starts to cry.

"OK, aquí está," Sra. Jaimes says before passing the phone to Daniela, who sounds breathless.

"Why do you sound like you were running?"

"My dad told me to hurry up since you were on the phone." There's a long pause as neither of us says what we're both thinking. "I'm really sorry you didn't make the team," Daniela finally says.

"Me too."

"You had it until the last question. It just had to be astronomy."

"My worst subject."

"Didn't you put up the stars?"

I stare at the plastic stars, noting the constellations Dad and I put up so I could study before I went to bed. Ursa Major is right above my eyes, with Ursa Minor due north by the wall's edge. Then Leo down to the left by the window and Gemini, Orion, and Taurus closer to the bathroom. Ms. Mackenzie gave us each a pack on the last day of school, and we both put them up in our rooms that night.

"They didn't help." I roll onto my side, tucking the pillow underneath my neck. "It's just so unfair. Boys get everything at our school. They get to wear and do whatever they want. They make the rules."

"But you heard Marcus, right?" Daniela says, the click of a closed door as she takes the phone into her room. "You can be the alternate."

I groan.

"I know it's not the same as actually competing—"

"I wouldn't even be technically on the team."

"But you'll still get to practice, and you'll be ready for next year when Marcus and Mikey are gone. It won't be the same without you."

I roll onto my back, starfishing across the bed. "What would I do every day at practice, besides listen to the boys call me Dress Code? I don't even know if I want to be on the team anymore."

I want to be on the team. I just don't want to be second best. A leftover. I don't want to be treated like I'm just a girl.

"If you do it, at least we would get to hang out. Otherwise, I'll be at practice all the time, and we'll never get to see each other. We only have Ms. Scott's and Ms. Anthony's classes together."

I know that, too. I'm not sure how we'll stay best friends if we only see each other three times a day.

"Please, Margie," Daniela says, and I can picture the pleading look in her eyes. "We'll study together so you don't get behind for next year. We can still be the Queens of Quiz. But only if you say yes."

The light-green plastic stars shine down at me. I didn't learn all these darn constellations for nothing.

And I can't imagine getting through sixth grade without Daniela.

"Fine. I'll do it. But I've got to get them to stop calling me Dress Code."

"Just don't get dress coded again! It's not hard. You can take some style tips from me. You'll never get dress coded in unripped jeans or basketball shorts." Daniela laughs, the sound of her voice one of my favorite things. "Or own it!"

"Maybe." I definitely don't want to be known for wearing awful gym shorts. I was thinking I'd be popular for my great brain or sense of humor.

"See you at practice tomorrow," she says. "Remember: Queens of Quiz."

I say goodbye, wishing we actually were.

The next day Daniela pushes me through Mr. Shao's door and into the first official Quiz Bowl team practice. Inside it smells like burnt popcorn, and most of the team is sitting around while Sean sets out the buzzer equipment. Mr. Shao is bent over his keyboard, the offending bag of popcorn on a stack of folders beside him. Elman and another seventh grader I don't remember are on their phones, and Jamiya is taking pictures of some question packets, probably for the team account. Last night I spent ten minutes brushing my teeth because I was staring at the perfectly happy team on Instagram. They must have taken the photo right after I left. I tried to ignore Daniela's huge grin, wishing she looked at least a little disappointed that I wasn't standing beside her.

"Dress Code!" Marcus calls from his perch on one of the desks. "Back to argue about our pal Martin Luther King...Junior?" All the boys laugh, and Jamiya rolls her eyes. I fight the sinking ship inside me. I will not go down.

"Just do it," Daniela whispers from behind me, and I take a step forward.

"You said I could be an alternate. I'm here to... alternate."

I stand tall, feeling confident today in an outfit I picked out to feel my best: skinny blue jeans, a rainbow top, and gold-sequined shoes that I found in my closet during the whole skirt-measuring incident. I am not Dress Code.

"My name's Margie," I say.

"Got it, Dress Code."

"Marcus," Mr. Shao calls as a warning, though he doesn't look up from his computer screen.

"Excuse me. Got it, *Margie*," Marcus says, stretching out my name with a grin.

"What do I do first?"

Mikey hops off his desk, handing me a stack of question sets with a smile that seems genuine. "Learn to be the best."

I frown and Mikey continues. "You have to be ready to replace any one of us at any moment. We each have specialties. Mine are generally history and sports with a focus on Supreme Court cases and tennis, baseball, basketball, and hockey. Marcus?"

Marcus looks up from his phone. "Science and math. Right now, I'm working on animal phyla and famous mathematicians. I'm also awesome at geometry."

"He is," Mikey says, giving Marcus a short round of applause.

The rest of the room goes around shouting out specialties—movies, World Wars I and II, Egyptian mythology, massacres and assassinations, American politics—the list goes on, and I realize I should have been writing all this down. I'll have to go back, member by member, and ask each one. Sixth graders José and Xavier say general areas like history and books, and of course astronomy, but Daniela just smiles. She knows I know her areas: literature (specifically historic children's and Shakespeare), government structures and international politics, famous women in history, and basic math through algebra. She can do almost all the math problems in her head. When they say "Paper and pencil," she just smiles.

"I have an idea," Marcus says, scribbling on a sheet of notebook paper. "Why don't you do an audit of the team? Mark down each question a person gets right with a plus sign, and a minus for each wrong answer. That way we'll know who's pulling their weight and who's not."

He hands me the sheet of paper, which lists the team members. I know the Kings and Daniela (obviously), and Jamiya, Sean, Elman, and José from third period. Oh, and Xavier. That's it.

"I don't know everyone's names."

Marcus surveys the team. "For this first round, I'll supervise. Elman, you'll read questions." Elman nods and moves to the podium between the tables. Marcus points to each person as he splits up the teams. "Sean, Caleb, Henry, and Kai: you're Team One." The boys take their seats. "Team Two: Mikey, Jamiya, Daniela, and you know Xavier."

Xavier smiles sheepishly at me. At least he's not smirking and rubbing his victory in my face. Marcus points to a row of desks behind the tables. "In the bullpen will be José and Deven."

After grabbing a pencil, I sit at one of the desks behind Daniela's table. She smiles at me, but I can see the fear behind her eyes. She wants to prove herself today, to make sure they know she deserves to be on the team. She gets this way every first day of school, any time we get a new teacher, constantly wanting people to know she's smart and capable. If I were closer, I would whisper something encouraging, but I don't want the boys to know that she's nervous. We have to stick together on this one. I scan the list of names again, writing down a description for each unfamiliar face.

Henry: Barcelona soccer jersey. Asian, maybe Korean. Cracks his knuckles.

Kai: Green tips. Quiet. Very sunburnt nose.

Caleb: Live Oak hoodie. White. Pencil twirler.

Deven: Turquoise braces. Thick golden coils. Always checking his phone.

"Ready, everyone?" Marcus asks, and before they can respond, he nods at Elman, who reads the first question.

"Toss-up number one. Inspired by fables from the Ashanti people of Ghana, this trickster uses his wit and cunning to defeat much larger creatures. Having two forms, human and arachnid, this mischief maker is one of the great folk heroes. For ten points—name this—"

A buzzer. Jamiya. "Anansi."

"Correct, ten points," Elman says, and I put a plus sign by her name. The three bonus questions flash by as I try to figure out how to mark responses when only the captain responds.

"Toss-Up number two. Pencil and paper ready."

Everyone's eyes drop to their papers. I decide to flip my paper over. No reason I can't practice, too.

"An architect needs to find the length of each side of a square whose area is the same as a rectangle whose width is eighty and whose length is twenty. By computing the area of the rectangle—"

A buzzer. Mikey. "Forty."

Elman nods. "Before the power mark. Fifteen points." I put a plus sign by Mikey's name.

Marcus gives him a high five. "Nice work, man."

The routine continues for the rest of practice. Mikey has the most correct responses, followed closely by Jamiya. A girl. But no one gives her a high five after her right answers. No one says "Nice work." Each time she answers correctly, Daniela and I smile, but the veteran boys don't care, while the new ones seem shocked that she knew the answer, as if they can't believe a girl is doing this well. Only Mikey nods at her after she answers, a small acknowledgment that she's killing it.

Daniela doesn't answer a single question, even the ones I know she knows. Maybe she's frozen because of nerves. She barely even contributes to the bonus question discussions. She's going to have to start showing off her skills if we're going to take over the crown.

I place a plus sign next to Sean's name. His first individual answer right. Within seconds, Marcus is giving him a high five. "That's my man, all up on his modern speeches! Four score and all that!"

That's my man. Ugh. This school is not made for girls.

chapter 8

WOMEN'S RIGHTS ARE **HUMAN RIGHTS.**
—HILLARY CLINTON

On Friday during second period, I split the back page in my math notebook into two columns. Girls on one half, boys on the other. Using Marcus's strategy to audit the Quiz Bowl team, I decide to audit my classes, boys versus girls. Boys get away with breaking the dress code. Boys run Quiz Bowl. I want to see if they dominate our classrooms, too. So far, Mr. De Leon has called on seven boys and not one girl. Not one. And it's not like we aren't raising our hands to answer the questions, because we are. This class has sixteen boys and fourteen girls spread evenly across the room. At first, I made a little grid where each person was sitting, *B* for boy and *G* for girl, but then it got too complicated. And I don't know everyone's name yet, except Xavier from Quiz Bowl, who is sitting in the front row next to the windows.

"Number seven," Mr. De Leon calls from his spot on the stool by the overhead projector. It's hard to see the screen with the bright light coming through the floor-to-ceiling windows, so Mr. De Leon writes in a superthick marker. He adjusts his tie, part of the standard guy teacher wardrobe of black pants, white shirt, black tie, and sneakers. "The missing factor is..."

My hand shoots up. I look around. Two other girls raise their hands. Four boys.

"Daniel," Mr. De Leon says, and I put another tally in the boys' column. "Nope, try again," he continues. I must have missed Daniel's answer. After an entire minute, Daniel finally guesses seven.

"No. Look at your multiplication table."

We wait while Daniel digs in his notebook. It should be glued to the cover. We did that the first day.

"Got it?" Mr. De Leon asks, and Daniel nods.

"Now find four and slide over until you get to sixteen."

Again we wait. I'm going to be an old lady by the time he answers this question.

"Four?" Daniel whispers.

"Correct." Mr. De Leon writes the answer in blue on the projection, taking a second to sip from a silver coffee mug printed with his name. "Number eight. The value of x is..."

Bam. My hand is back up. This time I'm the only girl. *Come on, girls. Get those hands up!*

"Margie."

What? I'm midtally in the boys' section, and I haven't even been paying attention to the questions, just raising my hand and putting down tally marks. My eyes scramble over the problem, the x and 32 and -7 and my answer.

"Three."

"No." Hands shoot up around the room. Wait a second. I look down at my page. Oh no, I read the wrong answer. I put my hand back up. "I'm sorry. I read the wrong—"

"James?"

"Thirteen."

"Correct."

I scratch a mark in the boys' column before abandoning my notebook and heading to the back of the classroom, grabbing the girl's pink bathroom pass off the hook. I have got to get out of here.

I slam my notebook down on the table next to Daniela when I get to Ms. Anthony's world cultures class. I've been waiting to talk to her for hours since she had a lunch bunch with her Spanish teacher today.

"I can't take it anymore!" I say, dropping into my seat.

Daniela doesn't respond right away as she's furiously writing out a toss-up question in her Quiz Bowl notebook, her lips mouthing the question as she frames it. I tap her shoulder. She holds up a finger. She flips back in her notebook and scans a page titled "Egyptian Mythology" before finishing her question. I read over her shoulder and only get "head of a jackal." I tap her shoulder again with a huff.

"Okay, sorry, what's wrong? Why are you freaking out?"

"I'm not freaking out!" I say, flipping past the colored-pencil maps in my notebook. "Okay. I'm freaking out, sort of, but for a good reason." I grab my boy-girl audit sheet, now full of tallies, each class written in its own pen color.

Daniela leans closer. "What is that?"

"It's an audit."

"What? Like from Quiz Bowl?"

"Exactly!" I say, tapping my two columns with the eraser on my pencil. "But instead of counting correct answers I'm tallying discrimination. And look. At. This!"

She scans the two columns, her braid falling over her shoulder onto her chambray button-up.

"Seriously?" Daniela says, turning back to her notebook.

"That's it? 'Seriously?' That's all you have to say?"

"I'm not trying to be rude, Margie, but this is my

first set of toss-up questions, and I have to get them right. I don't have time to look at your list right now."

"It's an audit."

"You know what I mean."

I scoot closer to her, my blue chair tilting. "You don't think girls being treated equally is important?"

"Of course I do," she says, back on her Egyptian mythology list to write another question. "But I'm actually dealing with this for real right now. You know I blew it the other day at practice, and Marcus and Mikey are going to be harder on me because I'm the only other girl. And I'm a sixth grader. You're using a lot of energy getting stressed out about who can wear shorts but you're not really doing anything. You're sort of just complaining."

I scoot back in my chair. "I'm not complaining; I'm gathering evidence."

"Okay, then. But it seems like a lot of time spent freaking out about this instead of trying to get back on the Quiz Bowl team."

Trying to get back on Quiz Bowl. Like I have any choice, like I can wish myself out of being the alternate.

"Fine. I won't talk about it anymore."

Daniela sighs. "You can talk about it, but can you just wait until I finish these? Then we can be angry together."

I smile. "Do you want me to read the ones you have done?"

She shakes her head. "I'll have Jamiya do it when we meet after school."

"But there's no practice today. Mr. Shao has a dentist appointment."

"I'm going to her house after school to work on Quiz Bowl stuff. She's going to review my toss-ups."

I try to hide my surprise. "Eighth graders never hang out with sixth graders."

Daniela shrugs. "We're the only two girls on the team...."

She must see my face because she pauses, reaching an arm to my shoulder. "I mean, you're on the team, too, but you know what I mean. It's different. And maybe you can come next time? I can ask her."

No way! How embarrassing to be the tagalong.

"Do you want some Skittles?" Daniela asks,

pulling a rolled-up bag of half-eaten Skittles out of her pocket. She always has candy; she loves Skittles almost more than Quiz Bowl. I hold out my hand as she drops in a few.

"You gave me red and orange? Those are your favorites."

She smiles and goes back to her Egyptian mythology, and I take out my class notebook, knowing Ms. Anthony will be starting class soon. The bright colors of Ms. Anthony's room do nothing to ease my frustrations. One wall is orange, another neon green, another purple, one yellow, as if she couldn't decide on a color and just threw them all up on the walls. Ms. Anthony stands behind her computer, fussing with the enormous TV it's connected to, grumbling at the remote. I actually heard her say a swear word the other day when I was sharpening my pencil near her computer. She didn't notice me.

"Okay, scholars," Ms. Anthony says, stepping away from the computer. Ms. Anthony is one of the most impressive women I've ever met: she graduated at the top of her class at UT Austin with *two* degrees: education and international studies. She runs the Austin marathon every year and is one of the youngest teachers. She's definitely the most fashionable. Today she's wearing a floral tunic over black leggings and a thick neon-yellow chain necklace. She's also one of the few Black teachers at our school. In an introductory slideshow, she told us about her Afro-Cuban family history and how she studied abroad in Japan for a year in college.

"Okay, scholars," she repeats because certain scholars weren't ready. "Look at this picture. Think about it. What do you see?"

On the board is a picture of a bunch of men who look how my grandpa Teddy would if he was still alive and—

"The president!" a student shouts from the back of the room. Ms. Anthony frowns. She calls on Sophia from my PE class. "Thanks for raising your hand, Sophia."

"The president and his government?"

"Close," Ms. Anthony says. "Daniela?"

"That's the president and his cabinet members."

Ms. Anthony smiles. "Yes. Take a minute to talk to the classmate across from you about what you see."

Daniela frowns, wishing we were partners, but I'm paired with William from our old elementary school. William is pretty smart, but he never looks up from his doodling, so he doesn't pull his weight.

"So? What do you notice?" I ask William, trying to be polite. He continues to scratch Sharpie scales onto a snake slithering up his notebook. I wait a few more seconds, hoping he'll glance in my direction. "Anything?" Nothing. "Obviously, I notice that it's mostly men, which seems super unfair."

William shrugs. Is that a response or a stretch?

"Thirty seconds!" Ms. Anthony calls.

"I also noticed—"

"All four ladies are smiling with teeth. Men have both teeth and no teeth showing. But women: all teeth."

"I don't think Ms. Anthony cares about teeth," I say, unsure what teeth have to do with anything. William hunches over his notebook again, sliding a red Sharpie over the snake's forked tongue. I wish Daniela could rescue me.

"Time!" Ms. Anthony calls, taking a seat on the tall red stool by the computer. "What do you see?"

She pulls a stick from her jar of Popsicle sticks with our names on them. "Juan Carlos."

"I see people dressed up fancy, mostly the men in suits and some ladies in skirts."

"Okay," Ms. Anthony says, swirling the sticks before pulling out another name. "Kaysie?"

"I see people smiling for an important picture."

Another stick. "William?"

Ha. Guess who should have been a better participant?

"All the women are smiling with teeth, but only some of the men are. Some of the men aren't smiling at all."

"That's a great insight, William," Ms. Anthony says, looking as surprised as I feel. I guess I underestimated him. "We'll have to come back to think about why women are smiling this way and the men aren't. Any other observations?"

Several hands shoot up around the room, including mine. "Margie?"

"Most of the people in the picture are men, which means that most of the people in charge of the government are men. At least the people picked by the president."

Ms. Anthony beams. "Yes, Margie. And is it unusual for the leaders of our country to be men?"

The class shouts no, me loudest of all. I know men run the world. I've seen the tallies in my notebook. I tap Daniela's shoulder and give her an "I told you so" look as I point to my audit. She smiles, shaking her head at me.

"It's definitely not unusual here in the United States," Ms. Anthony says as she rounds the back table, tapping a boy in a blue T-shirt who is reading a book under his desk. He quickly slams it closed, his eyes now glued to the screen. "You'll also notice that most of the people in the picture are *white* men, what we call 'intersectionality of privilege.' 'Intersectionality' is a word invented by a law professor named Dr. Kimberlé Crenshaw that describes how our identities—how we define ourselves, how others define us—are complex. For example, I'm Black *and* a woman. Someone might be an immigrant *and* have a disability. And all those parts of who we are affect how we're treated in society, and the power—or privilege—we have to make change. We're not diving into that topic just yet, but keep it in mind. So far, we've been talking about the basic components of a civilization or a culture, and today we're going to talk about who runs those systems: men, women, or both."

Ms. Anthony taps her computer, and a photo of older Asian women wearing red head wraps and long skirts appears. They each hold a gold bell or some metal instrument. "These are the Mosuo women of China's northern Yunnan province. They are one of the few matriarchal societies in the world. Their culture is changing with the addition of technology and increased global communication, but today we're going to study some of their practices, as well as some other women-led cultures."

As Ms. Anthony passes out articles about these different women, I start to picture it: a world run by women. Women presidents, women football coaches, women making laws and running meetings and standing in photos in the Oval Office smiling with teeth or no teeth. An all-girl Quiz Bowl team. Ms.

Anthony drops the article on my desk, and it covers my boy-girl audit, and even though I haven't added a single tally mark since her class started, if I did, the numbers would be even. I look down at the Mosuo women pictured in my article.

A women-led society here at Live Oak? Fat chance.

But then again...

chapter 9

A WOMAN'S PLACE
IS IN THE
RESISTANCE.

On Saturday, I hide inside the Macy's changing room, knowing in a few minutes Grandma will be pounding on the door, telling me to come out already, or tossing another hideous dress over the top. Thankfully, the lock on this room works. She barged in on me at Dillard's. "Nothing I haven't seen before," she said as she tossed me an ankle-length satin dress that I could have worn for my First Communion.

A pile of clothes teeters on the small stool and a few pairs of pants hang by the door. We're supposed to be shopping for clothes to replace the ones that are too short for school, but Dad told me I could get some other things if they "felt right." He said he had too much work to come with us (of course he did), so he gave me his credit card, which is tucked safely in the kitten wallet he got me for my birthday, right next to my school ID and a twenty-dollar bill I don't remember getting.

Boom, boom. Grandma's back. I spot her navy pumps under the door.

"Get goin', Margaret. We can't be here all day."

"Just a minute."

She rattles the handle. "I found some nice tops for you. Good for school. Good for church. And on clearance."

"Okay, I'll be out in a second. Go sit in the waiting area, please."

She huffs before heading back down the hall, and I scramble into a high-low skirt with blue polka dots and a floral print. It even comes with a built-in belt. Looking at myself in the mirror, I realize I'd probably love it if I was fully choosing it and not being forced to wear it because of the stupid dress code. I leave my white T-shirt on and head to where Grandma is waiting. I find her talking to a young salesperson behind the counter.

"This is ridiculous," she says, shoving a hideous sweater toward the woman's face. "Fifty-four dollars for a sweater for a little girl? She won't even wear it the next year. Who has money like this?"

"Grandma!" I yell, hoping to distract her with my outfit.

"It's not even nice fabric. Look at this." She moves the cardigan closer to the salesperson, who is backing up while still managing to smile. "This won't last one wash!"

I walk over and pat her arm. "Grandma, how about this one?"

She turns, her lips immediately pursing, highlighting the wrinkles around her mouth.

"That isn't a real belt."

I sigh. "Ignore that right now. Look at the skirt."

We haven't agreed on a single item yet. Everything is too expensive or too casual. Too ripped or too embellished. Dad can afford to buy me clothes that aren't on sale sometimes, but he doesn't think we should spend money when we don't have to. That's careless. I'm not trying to buy expensive clothes, but Grandma thinks anything that's not on triple clearance is luxurious. Even though she hasn't seen the price, I can guess what she'll dislike about this one.

"Why is it uneven like that? The front is so short and showing your legs." Grandma leans forward to touch the edge of the skirt, running the fabric through her hands.

"It's the style, Grandma. Didn't you see Taylor Swift wearing one last week? And the front is long enough, anyway."

"Looks short to me."

"It's not," I say, lifting the edge of the skirt and turning to point to the tiny blue line four inches above my knee. "I marked it this morning so I would know."

"Still..." She circles me, her arms crossed over her navy cardigan and embroidered white blouse. "That belt is plastic."

"I know! It's just fashion."

"I think we can find something nicer, maybe like that dress I gave you."

I head back toward the dressing room. "I can't wear a dress like that to school. I need skirts and shorts, Grandma. That's literally why we're here."

"You just try on the dress."

"Grandma, I don't—"

"It's so lovely."

"Fine!" I say, marching back to the dressing room. The door locked when I left, so I slide under the gap. I pull off the skirt and stick it in my keep pile, though I doubt I'll get out of here with anything that costs more than two dollars.

I groan before pulling Grandma's dress off the hanger, hoping we can get this over with and I can spend the rest of the day in my room on Netflix or studying my Quiz Bowl cards. The dress is too tight around my waist, and I can't get it zipped all the way up, but I have to show her. Looking like a vanilla cupcake, I sneak out to the mirrors hoping no one from school sees me. Thankfully Grandma is waiting in an overstuffed chair, digging for something in her purse.

"Here," I say when I get to her, holding my arms out so she can get the full effect.

"No, no!" she says instantly. "That neck is too low for a young girl."

"You picked it!"

She struggles to scoot forward in the overstuffed chair. "Let me see closer." She squints her eyes at me, before shaking her head. "We'll find something better."

"No," I say, already walking back toward the dressing room. "I don't want to shop anymore. I'll tell Dad I want to order online." That's what I should have done in the first place. I'll just wear what I have for now.

When I come out from the dressing room, Grandma Colleen is standing by the counter with a bag. *Oh no.* What did she buy? Dad's credit card is safe in my wallet.

"I got you these," she says, pulling out a pair of brown corduroy pants I definitely did not try on. "They were on sale. And these." Out come a plastic pack of lace-trimmed underwear. "Some new panties." Oh my gosh, I have to get her out of here.

"Let's go!" I sigh, hoping she doesn't find any more hideous items before we escape the mall. *Have a fun day shopping*, Dad said. Yeah. Right.

I never break rules. I never get up to sharpen my pencil in class without raising my hand. I make a list of even the smallest sins when I go to reconciliation at church, not forgetting a single jealous thought or eye roll at Dad. In first grade I peed my pants because my teacher said we couldn't use the bathroom during an assembly. I do what I'm told.

Until today.

On Monday morning when I look through my freshly folded piles of school-appropriate pants and skirts, including the hideous brown corduroy pants Grandma bought me, I make the decision to break the rules. It's been a week since my perfect skirt got swapped for the awful gym shorts, and I am not going to follow the dress code anymore when it only applies to girls. In school, they're always teaching us about freedom and fairness, and the dress code is not fair. I know Mom would never make me wear clothes I hate just to meet stupid standards. So I put on the gold-sequined miniskirt I wore for school pictures last year. Yes, "mini" is in its name. Yes, it is out of dress code. Yes, I'm wearing it anyway. Even if it means I get suspended.

Although I was able to sneak out to the bus without Dad or Grandma noticing my outfit, Daniela gives me quite the look when I walk into first period. "You're wearing your picture day skirt?"

"Yes, I am," I say as I grab a warm-up slip from the shelf by the door. Ms. Scott is back by her desk talking to a boy. My heart races, but I stay calm. I wore this skirt for a reason. I review the speech I've been rehearsing all morning, in the mirror while I brushed my hair, in the bathroom before class, where I practiced one final time.

"You know it's out of...," Daniela asks, and I nod.

"I know. I'm making a statement."

She laughs. "Okaaaay." She knows my history. In fourth grade, I was a vegetarian for four days after we visited an urban farm, but then I couldn't say no to chili and cinnamon roll day at school. I've not been great at making a statement. Until today.

Today, if Ms. Scott calls me behind her desk with the ruler in hand, I'm going to speak up. I won't stand silently like last time, trying not to cry, like it was my fault for wearing the perfect first-day-of-school skirt. No. I know exactly what I'll say.

Ms. Scott, I appreciate all you do as our teacher. Always start with a compliment.

But it is unfair that you are dress coding me for this skirt when you haven't dress coded the boys in our class for the same thing.

Then, a specific example. *Just last week, you did not dress code Dylan for his blue shorts, even though they were out of compliance.*

And then the finale. *Boys and girls should have the same rights, so I demand that you treat me fairly and allow me to wear this skirt.*

It's perfect, just like a speech should be.

The school bell rings and Ms. Scott claps her hands. "Good morning, ladies and gentlemen. Today's warm-up: If you could travel back in time, where would you go and what would you do? You have four minutes. Thanks for writing silently." She presses a finger to her lips and starts the timer.

I always know when I would go back. The year Mom got sick. She was thirty-four, and I was almost two, and I'm always disappointed I don't remember her. The information I have is more like an encyclopedia entry: Madeline Rose Kelly. Social worker and activist. Graduated college in her home state of Virginia. Allergic to bees. Stories Dad told me have turned into memories, but they're not really mine, like *his* photos that he's added to *my* scrapbook. My time travel also coincides with me somehow discovering a cure for cancer. Or at least getting her to a doctor sooner. I know I ought to use my one chance to prevent the Holocaust or stop 9/11, but honestly, I just want my mom.

"Margaret Kelly, will you please join me back at my desk."

It's time. Ms. Scott waits in her rolling chair, no ruler in her hand, but definitely a dangerous smile. I pause, taking a deep breath. I was ready for this, but suddenly the desire to be a good girl begins crawling its way up my throat. Daniela raises an eyebrow like, "I told you so."

Then I remember the tallies. Remember all the

boys at school getting what they want: to wear short shorts, to answer all the questions in class, to earn a spot on the Quiz Bowl team. My picture doesn't have to be like the president's cabinet, full of men running the show. My life can be more like the Mosuo women. The words of my speech flow through my veins, making their way from my brain to my tongue. I raise my chin, letting my skirt hike up as I walk. There is nothing wrong with my gold-sequined skirt. Nothing.

I stop opposite Ms. Scott's desk, and she wiggles her pointer finger for me to come around the side. Her hands rest on top of her pilled, black skirt.

"It looks like we have a problem."

"We do?" I try to sound confident, but my throat catches.

"I think you know," she whispers, leaning toward me. "You're a smart girl."

I stand in silence, unable to think of any smart-girl responses.

"I'm going to go ahead and write a pass to the in-school suspension room since this is your second time out of dress code."

"That's not fair!" I gasp, my anger rising to replace the fear of being in trouble.

"The first time is a warning," Ms. Scott says, raising her eyebrows. "But here you are again, out of dress code. I don't even need to bother measuring this skirt."

"Ms. Scott, I appreciate all you do as our teacher—"

"Focus please," Ms. Scott yells to the whispering class. She doesn't look at me as she searches for a functioning pen.

"But it's unfair that you're dress coding me for this skirt"—my voice is soft, softer than I want it to be, but I'm saying it—"when you didn't dress code the boys."

"Are you accusing me of sexism?" Ms. Scott asks, her pen frozen over a behavior slip.

"I'm just saying that I shouldn't be getting in trouble if Dylan—"

"We're not talking about Dylan. We're talking about you. You made the choice to focus on fashion instead of your academics. Don't you want people to notice your brain and not your body?"

More whispers spring up around us. Ms. Scott

turns. "Minds on your own work. We'll be sharing that warm-up in two minutes." She turns back to the behavior slip, completely ignoring me. I'm not giving up yet.

"Last week Dylan was wearing blue shorts, and they were way out of dress code, and you didn't say anything. What about his shorts being a distraction?" Ms. Scott's eyes grow to asteroids and steam escapes the top of her head like a solar flare. I continue, though I feel suffocated by her heat. "Boys and girls should have the same—"

"We are not having this conversation, Ms. Kelly," Ms. Scott says as she scribbles my name on the slip before checking a box. She hands it to me and I stare at the bright-red check mark next to "Dress Code Violation." It's on a list that includes things like "Physical Altercation" and "Rude to Adult." No way is my sequin skirt equal to fighting.

"Take this down to the front office. They'll walk you to in-school suspension. You can try again tomorrow." Ms. Scott gestures toward the door. For a moment, I feel a spark of the fire I had this morning. Maybe I will.

chapter 10

I'm so bored. When I first got to the in-school suspension room an hour ago I was petrified, waiting for the moment when the suspension monitor, Ms. Padilla, calls Dad. Over an hour of silent sitting has drained all the fear right out of me. The ISS room is bare except for a scattering of desks in uneven rows and one shelf of books that are so tattered and damaged they look a century old. Ms. Padilla sits behind her desk watching the security cameras for the main building hallways and occasionally shouting at the boys to her left to stop talking. In the corner of the room, one kid is working with a tutor, but the rest of us just sit here. Doing nothing. Nothing at all.

The room is full of the usual suspects—kids with their hoods up and glowers on their faces, a boy I saw jumping off the cafeteria table on the first day—and three other girls. I don't know why they're here, but given their shorts and one girl's tank top, it's probably dress code. I appear to be the only sixth grader and the only white girl. One girl with long wavy black hair is wearing jean shorts that she might have cut herself. She sits between her friends, her feet up on a desk and toenails peeping out of sandals (also not dress code; only closed-toe shoes allowed). She's clearly the leader, as the other two seem to wait for her every response.

One of her friends has jean shorts that don't actually look too short, but she is wearing a black tank top with thin (but not spaghetti) straps. She sits up super straight, like she's ready for a job interview, as she reads a library book. The other wears blue gym shorts that look like the extra-extra-small pair Nurse Angela offered me on my first dress code violation. She's wearing a Live Oak volleyball T-shirt with a giant ball in the middle. I bet no one on the team cares about her shorts. The girls whisper to each other in Spanish, and Daniela would be proud that I can understand a little bit of their conversation: something about lunch and a car and maybe an apple but also maybe a squirrel. Probably not a squirrel.

The leader stretches over her desk, her long arms flopping over the front, her hair creating a veil over her face.

"Gloria Cardenas," Ms. Padilla calls, and the leader lifts her head, looking through the veil of her hair. "Gloria, now!"

Gloria peels herself from behind the desk, her legs sticking to the plastic chair in the hot room. She takes her time walking.

"Who are we calling this time, Gloria?" Ms. Padilla asks, her fingers clacking on the computer keys.

"Call who you want. You know my mom works."

"Aren't you tired of spending your days in here?"

Gloria sighs. "You all put me in here. I'm fine with what I'm wearing."

Ms. Padilla shakes her head. "You know you can't wear those shorts to school. This isn't the beach."

"No offense, Miss, but it's ninety-five degrees outside. Seems beachy to me."

Good point. It is hot. Really hot. And what does it matter if her legs are showing?

"You're not going to be ready for high school if you spend your entire year in here," Ms. Padilla says, and Gloria snorts.

"Just because my shorts are tiny doesn't mean my brain is."

Ms. Padilla sighs, and Gloria walks back to her desk. She is so impressive. She wasn't like me this morning with Ms. Scott, my voice barely a whisper as I asked her for fair treatment like Oliver Twist asking for more gruel. *Please, sir, may I wear my shiny skirt?* Even with a prepared speech, I still couldn't get it out. But Gloria is bold. The right things popped out of her mouth without hesitation. I wouldn't be able to think of anything clever that fast. My brain isn't packed with cool responses; I've only stored random Quiz Bowl facts.

The fluorescent lights flicker.

"Margaret Kelly," Ms. Padilla reads from my pass.

I raise my hand.

She clicks a few things on her computer screen. "Let's call your dad."

He is going to be so mad. I've only gotten grounded twice in my life. Once for stealing candy and another time for making a scene at our neighbor's birthday party. I really wanted the purple goggles that came out of the mermaid piñata, but some little kid's mom grabbed them and I had a meltdown. Grounded in elementary school meant no TV and no going to Daniela's house. Grounded in middle school probably means no phone. Ugh.

Ms. Padilla eats a potato chip while the phone rings. And rings. A click. Hooray for voice mail and Dad being too busy to answer his phone! Normally I hate when he's too busy at work to answer my texts right away. For once, I'm grateful for his stupid Chicago job.

"Good morning, this is Ms. Padilla from Live

Oak Middle School. I'm calling to let you know that your daughter, Margaret, will be serving in-school suspension until you can come bring her a change of clothes. This is her second dress code violation."

She gives him the number to call her back.

"I guess you'll just have to wait," Ms. Padilla says. "You can go back to your seat."

I trudge back to my empty desk, filled with the weight of my failure and the fear of Dad showing up. Then I do something I would never ever do before I became a girl who broke the rules. I put my head down on my desk.

"Pobrecita," one of the girls whispers to her friends. "Quizás, es su primera vez."

I lift my eyes to see the girl in the Live Oak soccer T-shirt watching me. "Si es mi primera vez en... detención," I say, "pero no mi primero...dress code violation."

She smiles. "¿Hablas español?"

I tilt my hand back and forth. "Más o menos."

"¿Cómo te llamas?"

"Margie."

"Yo me llamo Alejandra," she says, handing me a

piece of gum wrapped in black foil. "But you can call me Ale."

"OK, gracias." Might as well break another rule while I'm in here. Two, actually. Talking and chewing gum.

"It's not so bad," she says. "Did you bring a book?"

"I brought my backpack, but I don't have any library books yet. Or assignments I can work on, except for a math worksheet."

The girl leans over to Gloria, who is sketching on thick creamy paper. "Gloria, dale papel a Margie."

Gloria looks up from her drawing, pushing long strands of hair aside like curtains. As she flips through the sketchbook for an empty page, I see a dozen portraits of celebrities. Some I don't know, but others I can name instantly. She drew some in pen, but most are in pencil.

"Those are really good," I say, speaking a little louder so she can hear me, but hopefully not loud enough to get caught.

Gloria nods. "I practice." She rips out a blank page, then removes all the dangling paper bits from the edge.

"Do you guys get dress coded a lot?" I ask.

Gloria shrugs as she adds curls to some woman's hair. "It's my first time this year, but in seventh grade it was at least once a week."

"Seriously?"

She shrugs. "No pues, but I'm used to it."

"I've only been dress coded a few times total," Ale says. "I hate being here; me canso de hacer nada."

"What time is it? Do you think it's third period already?" the girl reading the book asks. I didn't realize there wasn't a clock in here, and we're not allowed to check our phones.

"Wasn't that the tardy bell?" Gloria asks, adding a smudge to the woman's cheek.

"Ugh, that means I'm missing Forensics. I love that class."

"Quiet, girls!" Ms. Padilla calls from her desk. "Or I'll move you apart."

I stare at my blank sheet of paper, suddenly even more angry than I was in Ms. Scott's room. All I have for the next few hours is a blank sheet of paper and a worksheet on one-step equations. I missed the peer review of my short story and will have to make up my math quiz tomorrow. If I stay here all day, I'll miss the new song we're learning in choir and the start of my animation project in visual media. Because I got suspended, I won't even get to use my brain at Quiz Bowl. The other girls are missing their own classes, too, frog dissections and historical debates. Gloria can draw, but otherwise we have nothing. We're banned from learning because our legs and our shoulders—our whole bodies—are a distraction. But to who?

I unwrap my piece of gum and pop it in my mouth. Something has got to change.

chapter 11

I AM WOMAN.
HEAR ME
ROAR.
—HELEN REDDY AND RAY BURTON

After school I stand outside our black front door, even though it's like a sauna out here from this afternoon's sprinkle. I'm not ready to go in. I reach down and pull a leaf off the potted geranium we got Grandma for Mother's Day. I don't know how it's stayed alive this long, though the end seems near. Maybe it is for me, too.

When I finally open the door, I'm surprised to

find Dad sitting at the table typing on his computer, his UT Austin coffee mug on a coaster by his side. He's never home this early, especially with traffic. Then he looks up, and that is not the face I was hoping for: he got the voice mail.

"Nice skirt," he says, typing a few more things before turning in his chair to face me.

I slide my hand down the gold sequins and head straight to give him a hello hug, the thing he's always begging for, but his arms feel strange around me. He lets go, but still holds my hands and looks me in the eye.

"You got dress coded again."

I nod. Dad rubs his temples. "Let me get this clear. You knowingly wore a skirt we had already determined was too short for school and then had to spend the day at in-school suspension?"

"You could have brought me a change of clothes," I say, angry that he's blaming me when he was too busy yet again to answer his phone. Yes, I was happy at first when he didn't answer, but that was before I had to spend seven hours in ISS, my brain shriveling like a California raisin.

Dad's mouth drops open. That was the wrong thing to say. "Do not blame this on me, Margaret Kelly. I was in meetings this morning when Ms. Scott called—"

"Ms. Scott called you, too?"

"Yes, and Ms. Padilla, but you are responsible for your choices. I couldn't leave my meeting even if I wanted to, but you knew you would get in-school suspension if you wore that skirt. You have to live with the consequences."

"But it's not fair that I can't wear the clothes I want," I say, running my fingers along the bottom of the skirt. "The dress code is stupid. The teachers only care about what girls are wearing. A boy could probably wear a swimsuit, and no one would say anything. And haven't you always said that I shouldn't be treated any differently 'cause I'm a girl? Didn't Mom want me to be a feminist like her?"

Dad sighs, rubbing the back of his hand over his eyebrows. "You're probably right. A lot of rules aren't fair, and your mom would know how to coach you through this. You and I can work on how to fix these big societal problems, but you didn't change any-thing today. You just got in trouble."

He sounds just like Daniela. *You didn't change anything. You're not doing anything.*

Dad squeezes my shoulder. "Seems like you already received consequences at school, so there's nothing else we need to do at home, unless you have another miniskirt you plan on wearing."

I shake my head no, relieved that nothing worse is going to happen. I still have my phone. Dad turns back to his computer, father-daughter discussion apparently over.

My bedroom looks like a hotel again. The bed is made with the top of my pink polka-dot sheets folded over the comforter to make a cuff, the rest tucked so tight around the edges my feet will suffocate. On my pillow is a note in Grandma Colleen's loopy cursive: "Hospital corners, turned down, pillows fluffed." The pile of books and notebooks next to my bed is now a neat stack, the edges lined up perfectly. That note just says "Even." My pajamas aren't lying behind the door anymore, and above the laundry basket is a little sticky note pressed to the wall: "Dirty clothes here." Even the picture frames on my dresser have been lined up in a row. She must have cleaned before she left for five o'clock mass.

I walk over to the dresser, pulling out the top drawer to find what I expected: all my underwear folded into tiny squares, my socks rolled into little balls and sorted by color.

"Dad!" I call to the dining room. "Grandma's been in my room again!"

I pause. "Dad!"

"What?" he says, peeking around the door, his eyes scanning a piece of paper in his hand.

"She keeps going through my stuff."

Dad looks around my room. "She's just trying to help."

I can do it myself. Dad made me start doing my own chores at four, partially so I would become an independent woman, but also because Mom was gone and he couldn't do it all himself. I wouldn't mind Grandma helping me clean if she just stopped there. But she goes through everything! My carefully sorted bottles of nail polish. Every note from Daniela stashed in my nightstand drawer. Thankfully, I don't have a diary anymore. I have no privacy. At least she doesn't have my phone passcode.

"Maybe if you cleaned your room more often, she wouldn't feel compelled to do it for you," Dad says as he picks up a sticky note by the light switch that says "Leave room. Lights off." He presses it against the wall before heading back to his work. I sigh, pushing the drawer closed, not bothering to look in the others, where all my shirts will be folded into tight squares and organized by color instead of how I want them: in order of what I actually like to wear.

Then I see it: crammed behind my dresser is a white piece of poster board with crinkled corners. I pull it out, brushing off the dust bunnies before laying it across my bed. "I am woman. Hear me roar," it says in block Sharpie letters, a red-and-orange lion drawn so that the words are coming out of its jaws. I found it on the sidewalk as Dad and I made our way home from the Women's March in Austin last year.

Marching was scary and exciting at the same time. At first, I was just cranky: it was unusually hot, and we stood around for hours before the march even started. I couldn't imagine why Mom would willingly do this on her precious days off. Dad had packed snacks, but I ate those in about an hour. Once we started moving with the whole crowd of people holding signs and flags, kids riding in wagons, it felt real. It was more people than I've ever seen in one place. People were all over the sidewalks and the streets. Some people were even waving from the windows of the skyscrapers. I felt part of something, and suddenly I understood why Mom did it. My heart beat fast as the people around us started chanting. I didn't sing along. Neither did Dad. But we were doing it! We were part of it. I was officially a feminist. But as we walked down the street, I got nervous because even though all the marching and chanting was really cool, I could tell the adults were really upset. They weren't having fun marching, like in a parade. They were angry.

Angry like I am now. About the dress code. About how unfair it all is. I can't imagine two more years at Live Oak arguing about my skirts or fighting for a spot on the Quiz Bowl team. I want to stand in the hallway and scream like the girl at the march who stood with her arms behind her and yelled into the crowd.

That's what we could do! We could do our own protest at school. A march or something. I run to the dining room.

"Dad, can I borrow your iPad?"

He's squinting at his computer, his shoulders hunched in the way that will make him complain about his old age aches and pains tonight at dinner.

"What do you need it for?"

"Research."

"What class?"

I lean against the doorjamb. "Not for class, just a project."

He holds it out, not looking up. "I changed the passcode. It's your birthday."

I take the iPad to my room and close the door, plopping onto my bed. I type in my birthday and pull up Safari. In Google, I search "dress code protest." At the top are thumbnails of girls in T-shirts and shorts. No one really looks out of dress code except for a few girls in spaghetti-strap tank tops. I open one of the photos to see the girl's homemade shirt: "I am not a distraction." That's almost exactly what Ms. Scott said to me!

The first article: "Teens protesting high school dress code fight for right to go braless..." Wow. I didn't think bras had anything to do with the dress code. I just started wearing one last year, and it took forever to convince Dad to buy it. Everyone in fifth grade except for me and the new girl, Isabella, was already wearing a bra. Dad finally took me to the mall, and I picked out this perfect light-pink silk bra. I wasn't planning to protest wearing a bra, but maybe I should? Maybe true feminists don't wear bras. Or makeup. Or shave their legs. Dad wouldn't let me shave my legs yet, anyway. Not until eighth grade. Daniela only wears a sports bra, and she doesn't wear makeup or shave her legs. Is she more of a feminist than I am? I make a note to do more research.

I scroll down the rest of the articles to find kids all over the place—Canada, Montana, Chicago—all protesting their school's dress code. Most of them are in high school, though some are eighth graders, but I'm sure we could do it, too. One high school girl even got arrested for wearing her protest shirt.

I'm not ready to get arrested. But I am ready for this.

I grab a notebook out of my neat stack, sending the rest askew. On a new page, I write "Live Oak Middle School Dress Code Protest To-Do List" and draw a line under it. I scroll back through the pictures, getting ideas for my plan.

1. Get a slogan
2. Tell girls about it (and boys if they want to join)
3. Pick a date
4. Make signs and shirts
5. Protest!!!

I can't wait to tell Daniela tomorrow at school. *You're just complaining*, she said. *You're not actually doing anything.* It's not a perfect plan yet, but it's a start. I might not be able to change everything sexist in the world, but wait until she sees this!

chapter 12

The wooden door to Mr. Shao's room slams behind me as I race into Quiz Bowl practice the next day. I trip over the backpacks strewn among the desks as I make my way over to the windows where Daniela and Jamiya are working. Daniela and I haven't had a chance to talk all day with pretests and lunch groups, and I'm desperate to show her my plans.

"You're late, Dress Code," Marcus calls over the

top of Elman's question. His hand slams the buzzer. *"Lord of the Flies."*

"Correct," Elman says, and starts another question. I drop my backpack beside Daniela and pull out my brand-new folder stuffed with the research I just acquired at the library.

"I didn't think you were coming," Daniela says, setting down her pile of practice cards. "I almost told them you were sick, but then if you showed up, they would know I lied."

"You better take practice seriously if you're hoping to make the team next year," Jamiya says as she shuffles through her own set of cards. "You already missed last practice because you were in ISS."

"You told her!" I whisper to Daniela.

"Jamiya doesn't care."

"You think I haven't been dress coded before?" Jamiya says, her eyebrows raised. "I'm Black. All the girls of color at this school get dress coded at some point, no matter what they're wearing." Her current outfit looks like it's in dress code: a black-and-white NASA T-shirt and a pair of galaxy-printed shorts. It's hard to tell because she's sitting down, but they don't look too short. But who knows what length actually makes Ms. Scott get out her ruler. Apparently it wouldn't matter how long they were anyway.

"Have you ever been sent to ISS?" I ask.

Jamiya shakes her head. "No, but that's just because my parents made a fuss the first time I got in-school suspension for dress code, and it hasn't happened since."

Dad would never make a fuss at school. He doesn't even make a fuss when they get his order wrong at a restaurant. Besides, he couldn't bother to answer the phone when I got dress coded, let alone come get me out of in-school suspension.

"Can we get back to the practice set?" Daniela asks. "We only have thirty minutes left."

"Let me show you something first," I say, glancing at Mr. Shao, grateful to see he's staring at his computer, headphones on. I quickly lay out the series of articles about dress code protests like they're contraband. "I've been doing research. Look!"

I hand Daniela the first article, the one with the girls and the homemade "I am not a distraction"

T-shirts. "See? Girls all over the place are protesting. And boys, too."

Daniela's silent as she takes the article from me. She twists the end of her braid as she reads. Jamiya grabs another article.

"At this march they got, like, four hundred kids to dress up," I say, pointing to one article, then another. "This one is just a girl by herself, but she made the news because her mom posted about it on Facebook."

"Quiet backstage," Elman yells.

"Look," I whisper, pointing to the major one. "This girl even got arrested for her protest."

"That's a little extreme," Daniela says, pushing the papers back at me and returning to her flash cards.

"It's brave! She's out there doing something and not just complaining. Right? Isn't that what you said I should do?" I slump back in the desk, my feet sliding across the stained floor.

"Did that girl getting arrested even change anything?" Daniela asks.

"I don't know. But I am going to do something about the dress code. A protest or something. You know it's unfair."

Jamiya lays her article down on the desk. "You know the dress code isn't the only unfair thing at this school, right? I can name a million: Marcus and Mikey are the only other Black kids in any of the advanced classes. Student Council has been fighting for three years to get more diverse books in the library. There's no gender-neutral bathrooms. Not to mention the millions of microaggressions: pronouncing kids' names wrong, telling us 'You don't sound Black.'"

"Ms. Johnson called me Danielle all last week," Daniela says with a roll of her eyes.

"And this is the first year I'm not the only girl on Quiz Bowl," Jamiya adds. "And now there's *two*."

Well, three, if you include me.

"This school does mistreat girls. I should show you my audit," I say.

Daniela puts her hands on mine to stop me from digging in my backpack. "Honestly, Margie, I don't get why the dress code is such a big deal to you. You were only dress coded twice, and one time it was on purpose."

"Yes, but you have no idea how embarrassing it was, standing in front of the class getting my skirt measured. And having to wear those stupid shorts. And ISS! Everyone knows me as Dress Code now. I'm not Margie. I'm Dress Code, all because of a stupid skirt."

Tears catch in my eyes, and Daniela squeezes my hand.

"I didn't realize you were so upset about it."

"I've been talking about it since the first day of school!" I shout.

"Quiet," both Mr. Shao and Elman warn, their heads snapping toward us.

I lean in closer. "But it's not just about me getting dress coded. When I was in ISS, I realized all these girls were missing school because of their clothes. We have to do something."

"But are you sure protesting is the right thing?" Daniela asks, swiping back a strand of hair. "Think about it like this: you know how new teachers or subs sometimes talk to me really slowly, with huge facial expressions because they think I don't speak English?"

I nod. I've seen it happen. "And then they're surprised when they hear you talk?"

"Exactly. The way to change their minds isn't to complain about it—it's to prove them wrong. Like my dad did with his real estate business. People didn't think a Mexican American man from a small border town in the Rio Grande valley could be successful in Austin, but now he's one of the top agents in the city. That's why I work so hard to be good at school and make it on the Quiz Bowl team. You think Marcus and Mikey aren't fair to girls because they're sexist? Well, prove them wrong by studying and getting better."

"How am I supposed to prove to Ms. Scott that my skirt isn't a distraction besides wearing more short skirts and asking everyone in class if they can still learn?"

Daniela laughs. "You would totally do that."

"You need a hashtag," Jamiya says. "If you're going to try to do a protest like one of these, you need something catchy for Instagram. That's the only way people are going to show up."

I didn't realize she was still reading the articles, but she has several on her desk.

"Yes, definitely," I say. "I've been thinking about a symbol, too, or a slogan, like these girls have. We could march maybe, or hold signs outside the school. Maybe you could help me with—"

Jamiya shakes her head. "I've got high school applications coming up, but get your ideas together first, and then I can help with your social media."

"That would be awesome!" As one of the popular eighth graders, she knows all the kids at school. She could really make a protest happen. "See, Daniela? Jamiya's in."

"I'm in-ish," Jamiya says as she picks up a stack of flash cards. "Like I said, I have my own changes I'm trying to make at Live Oak right now with Student Council. Besides, it is practically impossible to get Mr. Franklin to change his mind on anything." She flies through the cards faster than I could even read one, her mouth forming answers with each flip.

"So will you do it?" I ask, needing Daniela to say yes. I can't do this without her.

"I still think there might be a better way, but—"

"Yes!" I throw my arms around her shoulders, my desk tilting so it clangs into hers.

"Dress Code," Marcus calls from his seat at the front table, "come read these last few questions since Elman has to go." Finally, an official duty at practice, but now I just want to talk protests with my best friend!

"Dress Code!" Marcus yells again. "You're the alternate, so alternate."

I rush to the front of the room and almost trip again, this time over someone's saxophone case. Elman leaves the questions on the podium, and I note the purple pen marks beside the ones he's already asked. Four left. Standing in front of the tables full of boys, all their eyes on me—me, Dress Code, Margie—I feel a swell of power. I can do this. I can moderate this team of power-hungry boys, and I can run a protest, too.

"Toss-up. This senator was barred from speaking during debate after reading aloud a letter from Coretta Scott King. Senate majority leader Mitch McConnell employed Senate Rule Nineteen, stating that she had 'impugned the motives and conduct' of fellow senator and nominee for attorney general, Jeff Sessions. McConnell later defended the action, saying, 'She had appeared to violate the rule. She was warned. She was given an explanation. Nevertheless, she persisted.' For ten points, name this—"

A buzzer lights up. And so do I, realizing even famous women like Elizabeth Warren are speaking up and demanding respect.

Nevertheless, she persisted. And I will, too.

chapter 13

GIRLS WITH
DREAMS
BECOME
WOMEN WITH
VISION.

Blood rushes to my head, my feet propped above me, my legs parallel to Daniela's against my light-green wall. We've been lying on the bed like this so long that my toes prickle. It's our monthly Saturday sleepover, though we usually convince our parents to say yes to more. Especially since they can save a drop-off trip and return us at mass. We're supposed to be picking a movie to watch so we can "start settling down," but Daniela's doing impressions and I can't stop howling.

"Do another one!" I shout. "Do Father James!"

Father James was the priest at Saint Mark's when we got our First Communion. Daniela taps her unpainted toes against the wall, then stretches her hands in front of her like she's holding the tin of hosts. She bends her shoulders and raises her eyebrows.

"Boat-y of Christ," she says, her voice singsong as she hands out fake hosts. "Boat-y of Christ."

I start giggling again. "Do someone from school! Do Ms. Scott! Or the Kings!"

She shakes her head, the tips of her loose hair brushing the carpet. "I don't know any of those yet."

"Just try it! Marcus or Mikey would be easy. 'Hey, Dress Code, dust the buzzers!'"

"You've never had to clean anything," Daniela says, sitting up to put her hair back in a braid.

"Girls," Dad calls, knocking twice before pushing the door open. He peeks around the corner, already dressed in his University of Texas T-shirt and plaid pajama pants even though it's only nine o'clock on a Saturday night. "I can hear your giggles all the way across the house."

I point to Daniela. "It's her fault."

Dad smiles. "Impressions?" Daniela nods. "Let me guess, Father James?"

"Boat-y of Christ," we all say together, and even Dad chuckles.

"Okay, well, good night, girls. Don't stay up for hours practicing your Quiz Bowl questions, either." Dad leans over to flick on the jellyfish night-light by my desk. "I know you're Queens of Quiz, but you need to save your skills for when you're both onstage, slamming those buzzers."

Daniela side-eyes me, and I shake my head.

"Got it! Night, Dad."

He yawns as he pulls my door closed. Daniela pounces. "You didn't tell your dad you're not on the Quiz Bowl team?"

"I am on the Quiz Bowl team."

"You know what I mean." I tuck the pillow behind my head and stare up at the stars. "Margie?"

"No, he doesn't know that I'm the alternate, but

it doesn't matter. He's going to miss all the actual meets for work anyway."

Daniela frowns. "Does he know about the dress code and your protest idea?"

"Uh, no. Definitely not."

"He's going to flip if he finds out."

"I know," I say, reaching for the notebook on my side table. "Which is why he's not going to know. So, shh. We're going to have to whisper if we want to actually plan this protest."

"I'm not sure I actually do."

"You already said yes, and I have the plan right here." I turn to the list I started Monday. "I've been doing more research, and some girls actually changed things at their schools."

"But what exactly are people going to do? Walk out of class? Wear short skirts?" Daniela asks. "I love you, but there is no way I'm wearing a miniskirt."

"We'll have to figure that out. For now, let's start with something easy like the Instagram account."

I grab my phone off the charger. Dad let me keep it in my room tonight since he thought we'd want to spend all our time taking selfies. Daniela hates selfies.

"Doesn't your dad check your phone?"

"He used to all the time, but he's so busy with work he barely checks it anymore. I put a tissue on it the other night so I could tell if he moved it, and he hadn't."

"That is so not like your dad. Is this all because of his new job?"

I nod. "I guess so. It's a lot of stress now that he's a manager."

Daniela tilts her head. "Does it bother you? That he's sort of ignoring you."

I force a smile as a pang ripples through my chest. "At least I don't have to worry about him finding out about our plans."

Daniela frowns and pats my arm. "Are you making a new account or doing it under your personal one?"

"A new one," I say, opening Instagram. "Just in case. I'm going to search 'feminist' for names and see what comes up." After a few seconds I read, "Feministfightclub, feministwarrior, FeministFabulous, feministvoice, feminist.ashley, feminist—"

"Does it have to have 'feminist' in the name?"

"How about FutureFeministsofLiveOakMiddle?"

"Aren't you already a feminist?" Daniela asks, folding a pillow under her arms.

"FeministsofLiveOak?"

Daniela shakes her head. "That's way too long."

"LadiesofLiveOak?"

"That sounds like we're having a tea party," Daniela says. "This whole thing is about the dress code, so why not something with that?" Her fingers drum along her legs as she thinks. "CodeBreakers?"

"Ooh, I like that!" I say. "It's not so obvious, but also awesome."

"It could get confused with something else, though," Daniela argues, twisting the end of her braid. "Like the code breakers during World War II or the Navajo code talkers." Leave it to Quiz Bowl girls to get nerdy about a name. I type it into Instagram.

"CodeBreakers is already taken anyway. How about LiveOakCodeBreakers?"

"I like it," Daniela says with a yawn. I reach over to high-five her.

"You didn't even want to be a part of the protest,

and now you helped with the hardest part: the name!"

She laughs. "I don't think picking a name is going to be the hardest part."

I cross "Instagram account" off the to-do list. "What should our first post be?"

Before she can answer, it hits me. "I know exactly!"

I hop off the bed, bumping Daniela, who was taking a drink of water. "Ack, careful, Margie!"

"Sorry," I say as I race to the closet, swiping through the properly measured dresses and skirts until I feel the tulle in my hands, the sequins along the edge: the perfect first-day-of-sixth-grade skirt. The skirt that started it all.

"Get off the bed," I tell her, and she rolls off, leaning against the wall. I spread the floral comforter smooth before laying the skirt in the middle of the bed, straightening the edges and fluffing the layers.

I pull over my desk chair and stand on the seat, the chair wobbly on my plush carpet. I center the skirt in my phone screen, hoping the sequins pick up the light. I take several photos before showing Daniela.

"I'll add a filter, and then we'll post it with this caption: Does this skirt look like a distraction to you? Plus our own hashtags."

"That is good," Daniela says as she crawls back into bed. She watches as I edit the photo. The sequins and the flowers on my bed really pop with the Lo-Fi filter. Butterflies flood my stomach.

"Are you really doing this?" Daniela asks, her eyes as worried as I feel.

For a moment I wonder what Dad would say if he found out. What my mom might say. Would she be proud of me for standing up for myself? I hope so.

We look at the picture: a skirt that shouldn't have been remarkable, that shouldn't have caused a protest. It's just a skirt. "Do you think this will actually work?" I ask. "Should I do it?"

My finger hovers over the button. Daniela smiles. "Post it."

chapter 14

SILENCE IS NOT AN OPTION.

It's been over a week, and we only have seventeen likes on our Instagram post, and all the comments are from me. Daniela and I tried talking to some girls we know from elementary school, but they were all afraid to get in trouble. And none of them had even gotten dress coded yet, though they'd all seen me in the gym shorts. Or at least heard about it. We need to start recruiting people, but outside the few kids from elementary and the Quiz Bowl team, I don't really know anyone here at Live Oak. I've been so obsessed with the dress code that I haven't bothered to make new friends. And I guess I didn't really worry because I had my best friend, Daniela.

At least I thought I did.

Across the room, Daniela and Jamiya are hunched over Jamiya's phone, both of them reading with squinted eyes before writing something in matching notebooks. They're just extra notebooks Mr. Shao gave the team from his closet, but they match. And I didn't get one because I'm the alternate. Jamiya points to something, and they both start laughing. Last year during Quiz Bowl, I could make Daniela laugh so hard she would start coughing whenever I did my buzzer dance, mostly me just slapping my hands around and humming whatever song came to my head. Whenever we got bored with studying, she'd yell, "Buzzer!" and I'd start dancing. She isn't laughing that hard now, but still. Even with her help on the protest, things feel different.

The whole team is in research mode for the first thirty minutes of practice, and while a projected timer runs down on the chalkboard, I've been setting up the buzzer system. Everyone is silently working on their phones or one of Mr. Shao's Chromebooks. Strangely, Mr. Shao is the only one making noise, singing along off-key to the music on his headphones.

"What are you guys looking at?" I ask Daniela and Jamiya when I finish with the buzzers. They don't respond. "Daniela? What is it?"

Daniela tugs on a cord and pulls out an earbud.

"We're watching this video about Brexit. You know, the United Kingdom leaving—"

"I know about Brexit," I say, even though I don't really. I just know the word sounds like those Hollywood mash-up names Grandma has memorized. Jamiya keeps watching the video, writing a few notes every few seconds, her deep-purple nail polish the same color as her pen.

"We still only have seventeen likes," I tell Daniela, pulling out my phone to show her the posts. "We have to get more girls involved or it won't work."

Jamiya reaches over and grabs my phone. She frowns at the screen. "Cool shot, but this doesn't even say what you want people to do."

"We haven't really decided that yet," I say, realizing now how stupid it is to start a protest without actually having a plan.

Jamiya scoffs. "That should be your priority, then. You have a hashtag?"

I nod.

"And only seventeen likes. How many followers do you have?"

"Only a few on this account," I say, embarrassed to admit that my personal account doesn't have many more.

Jamiya scrunches her eyebrows. "You need someone with followers to share it, someone popular." She hands the phone back to me. "No one is going to risk ISS for sixth graders. But if you could find someone else to post about it, you might get more people involved."

"Would you—" I ask, and Jamiya shakes her head before I can even finish.

"I'm not the right person for this. I've only been dress coded once, but there are some girls who live in ISS because of the dress code. Who knows, maybe one of them is already planning a protest of her own."

"Thanks," I say, wondering how a sixth-grade Quiz Bowl alternate who barely knows anyone's name is going to get a popular girl to support a protest. There are over a thousand kids at this school. Then I remember Gloria and the other girls from ISS. Gloria said she gets dress coded all the time, and from the few times I've seen her in the hallway since, she's definitely popular enough to be our spokesperson.

"Can I help you guys with research?" I ask, sitting down beside them. Daniela shakes her head before handing Jamiya's earbud back to her.

"We're actually going to go do some research in the library."

"I can go with you. I can work on some new post ideas while we research."

"No," Daniela says. "We really need to focus on Quiz Bowl, and we already know what we're working on. Besides, aren't you helping Marcus with buzzers when research is over?"

Bright-red numbers count down the final two minutes. Daniela tucks her matching notebook in her backpack before zipping it up. My throat tightens as I watch her prepare to walk away from me.

"See you later," Daniela says, and as the numbers count down, I feel a bit like they're counting down the seconds until I'm no longer Daniela's best friend.

chapter 15

GIRLS JUST
WANNA HAVE
**FUNDAMENTAL
RIGHTS.**

"Please, Daniela, come with me. It won't take long," I beg. Daniela marches a few steps ahead of me on her way to world cultures, her shoulders turning, her body curving as she slides through the crowded halls. "It will take two seconds to tell her about the protest. If she's not interested, we'll come straight back to school."

"I have Quiz Bowl," she says, yanking the bottom

of her backpack strap to tighten it. Without thinking, I pull on mine, too.

"*We* have Quiz Bowl. Just tell the Kings you're meeting with a teacher."

Daniela turns to me with a look of horror. "I can't say I'm at tutoring! Quiz Bowl kids do not need tutoring. Ever."

I sigh. "Fine, then say that it's not for tutoring, but an award or something. Please, Daniela. 7-Eleven is right across the street. It won't take more than ten minutes."

"What makes you think she'll even say yes?"

"She might not, but she said she gets dress coded all the time. She's got to be fed up. And we at least have to try. This protest is going nowhere without an eighth grader on our side."

Daniela gets a drink from the water fountain, her ponytail sliding over her shoulder. She stands up and flicks it back, staring at me as if she's trying to solve a puzzle and I'm the clue.

"I still don't get why you need me to go with you. You said you talked to Gloria and her friends when you were in ISS."

"I'll seem like a weirdo if I go by myself. It'll be more convincing if there's two of us."

"Can't we go some other time? Before school or something? I really don't want to miss practice."

I shake my head. "I don't know when she gets here in the morning, but she goes to 7-Eleven after school. They were talking about it that day in ISS. Please, Daniela."

"Fine," she says, turning the handle to Ms. Anthony's room. "But we have to be fast."

After school I wait for Daniela right outside the school doors while she turns in an assignment for math. Kids push past me, already grabbing the contraband out of their backpacks—chips, candy, phones—as they head toward the buses. The breeze blows the hair off my cheek, and I'm grateful for the momentary break from the heat. I'm sweating because I'm nervous and because it's over a hundred degrees. No wonder girls want to wear shorts and skirts. September in Texas is like walking on the sun.

"Let's go!" I say the moment I see Daniela, no time to waste.

"Hold on, everybody!" our crossing guard, Officer Dominguez, shouts as she blocks our path, her voice too big for her body. She moves to the center of the street and waves us across with flags. Behind us a flood of kids heads for the 7-Eleven. The owner must be a millionaire.

The doorbell rings as we enter, and there's already a line of kids down the counter past the hot dogs and the coolers of energy drinks. Gloria's not in line, which is actually better since it would be weird to talk to her while she was waiting to check out.

"Is she here?" Daniela asks, and I shrug, looking down the first aisle. "What's the plan when we find her? 'Hey, Gloria, do you get dress coded a lot? Want to join our protest?'"

"I don't really have a plan, but that works!"

"Margie! We're going to sound like stupid sixth graders." Daniela marches toward the coolers.

"Trust me. I'll think of—"

Suddenly I spot Gloria at the end of the candy aisle. "That's her!"

"I cannot believe we're doing this," Daniela mutters as I pull her toward Gloria. She is scanning the chocolate bars when we approach.

"Excuse me, Gloria?" I say, and she turns with a confused look.

"Yeah..."

"Hi. I'm Margie. We met in ISS a couple weeks ago?" Gloria tilts her head. It seems to take her a minute to recognize me. Daniela elbows my ribs. "This is my friend, Daniela."

They both say hi and wait for me to keep this awkward conversation moving.

"I know this is weird coming up to you, but we're working on this project, and we need your help."

Gloria raises an eyebrow. "Help with what?"

"You said you've been dress coded a bunch of times, right?"

She nods, slowly, twisting quarters between her fingers. "So?"

She's wearing a cropped white blouse over army-green cargo pants ripped at the knees. I wonder if she got dress coded today. Even if she didn't, I know what the adults at school would be thinking: her clothes are inappropriate. She doesn't look "ready to learn." She's a distraction. But she looks confident to me. And tough. And also beautiful, but that's just an afterthought.

"Does it bother you that you get dress coded all the time?" I ask, leaning against the shelf of peanuts and trail mix.

Gloria shrugs. "I'm used to it."

"You're way braver than I am because spending seven hours in detention doing nothing was awful. Not to mention the gross gym shorts. It's been bugging me ever since that girls get dress coded way more than boys at our school."

Gloria scoffs. "Yeah, I know. That's been happening since I was in sixth grade."

"Right! And we want to do something to change it."

Gloria looks at me and then Daniela. "Like what?"

I turn to Daniela for some encouragement, but she just looks at me like "Go ahead, this is your big idea."

"We want to do a protest. Like a walkout or a march." I grab my phone to show her the Instagram account. She leans forward to look at the picture. "We're using #LiveOakCodeBreakers as a hashtag."

"No manches, walking out of class will get you written up. You'll get suspended," Gloria says, crossing her arms.

"We know," I say, trying to sound more confident than I feel. I haven't really let myself dwell on the consequences.

"For something big like a protest, you might even get sent to ALC," she adds. The alternative learning center. I heard about it when I was in ISS. Only the kids who've committed major crimes get sent there. It's like boot camp and school mixed together. Gloria assesses me, probably wondering what I wonder all the time: Am I brave enough to do this?

"If it happens, it happens," I say, and she half smiles as if she only half believes me.

"So what do you need me for?"

Daniela steps forward. "We're having a hard time getting girls to join us because we're sixth graders, and we don't know that many people yet, and honestly, we're sixth graders—"

"And, mija, you need me to help get people to do your protest?"

"It would be *our* protest, then," I add. "There's not a lot of time for things to change before you go to high school, but we could really use your help. If you want to. You can think about it. We're on Instagram."

Daniela grabs my elbow. "And now we have to go because we're late for practice, but thanks for listening."

"Yeah," Gloria says, a bemused smile on her face. She grabs a Milky Way as Daniela and I burrow into the crowd of students clutching their snacks. I'm feeling good, hopeful but not certain, but also, I'm super sweaty from being nervous and hot. Outside, the streets are full of cars waiting for pickup.

"I think she might actually say yes," Daniela says as we wait for the crossing guard to let us back across the street. Finally, she waves the flags, her whistle blowing three short bursts at the car speeding down the street.

"I hope so."

"Now we need to run so we're not even more late!"

"Beat you there!" I yell as I take off running down the sidewalk, certain Daniela will be by my side in seconds.

It comes in the middle of practice. While I'm taking a break from printing out new question packets on Mr. Shao's dusty old computer, I get it. A new Instagram follower: @GlowGirl13. Daniela is in a practice round, her back to me. I whisper her name while Marcus flips through the cards. She doesn't turn.

"Daniela!" I shout a little louder, and she flips around.

"What?"

I hold up my phone. "It's Gloria!"

She mouths "cool," but I can tell she's really thinking "Not right now."

A couple of seconds later my phone buzzes. A notification of a message from GlowGirl13.

I hide my phone under the desk and peek over my shoulder, just in case Mr. Shao decides to enforce the school's no-phone policy. I confirm that he is still hanging up some student-made posters about World

War I on the wall across the room. I open my Instagram to see the message: **Dress I wore last week. Third time dress coded this year.** Then, a photo of her in a tall mirror. She's wearing a black-and-white-striped T-shirt dress with the sleeves rolled up past her elbows. The curved hem of the dress is a few inches above her knees: short, but too short? "Let's do it" is scrolled across the picture in lime-green writing.

I send her a message. **Really?**

Por que no? she types again. **What's the plan?**

Right. We need a plan.

Working on it. Let's talk tomorrow?

Ok, Chica.

I set my phone down, realizing for the first time that this idea isn't just in my head anymore. It's not just Daniela and I scheming from my bedroom. Gloria knows, and soon the whole school will hear about it, too. It's happening.

I hope we're ready.

chapter 16

Gloria is the baking soda to our vinegar-filled volcano. Once she joined, the protest erupted, pictures and comments and followers flowing around the school like magma. We're up to one hundred followers on Instagram, and now I hear whispers about it at lunch and in the girls' bathroom. Instead of laughing at the girls in the oversize T-shirts or gym shorts, people are angry, grumbling about the teachers and Mr. Franklin, our principal, as they pretend to complete assignments. Girls have even started sharing our new hashtag: #brainsnotbodies.

Gloria's been livestreaming the different outfits she's been dress coded in, commenting on why she liked the shirt or where she got the pants, telling the true story of the clothes and her fashion sense and not the one the school forced on her: that she was trying to be sexy, that she was focused only on her looks and not her education. Other girls have started sending us photos of themselves in their dress code outfits. It's how we got the idea for the actual protest. In just over a week, we're all going to walk out of class, changing into or revealing one of the outfits we had on when we got dress coded. People like Daniela, who've never been dress coded, can wear whatever matches their style because it's not about wearing short shorts. It's about wearing what we want.

Since Mr. Shao is out of the room making copies, the boys are louder than normal as they finish a second round of questions in preparation for tomorrow's preseason match. Elman leaps out of his chair anytime his team gets an answer right. At one point, Marcus puts Mikey in a headlock. Daniela and Jamiya quiz each other on the latest question set while they wait their turn. No one bothers me as I scroll my phone.

Hazlo! Gloria sends again. **No temes los haters.** She's been trying to get me to livestream, but I'm too embarrassed to talk on camera. On the Quiz Bowl stage, I know what kinds of things I'm going to get asked, but on a livestream, I just have to go with the flow, and I don't flow. That's what makes Gloria so great.

But I'll be terrible! You're so relaxed. I'll just send a photo of me in my other dress code skirt.

Si puedes! Just talk and be yourself.

That's much easier when you're an eighth grader with a ton of confidence.

"You've gone viral," Sean says as he slides into the desk beside me. I flip my phone over, hiding the chat, though I'm not sure why I'm suddenly so embarrassed that he saw it. I want people to see it. "It's really cool what you're doing. The dress code is trash. Look."

He gestures toward the boys at the front: at least two have shorts that are questionably above their knees. He's not telling me anything I don't already know. Even though I don't respond, he keeps going.

"I'm going to do it. Walk out with you guys. I heard about it from some of the eighth-grade girls, but I didn't know it was you who started it. I thought it was that girl Gloria."

"Gloria's done almost all the posts," I say, looking over at his clothes: khaki shorts and an orange T-shirt both safely within the dress code guidelines. "How'd you know it was me who started it?"

"Jamiya told us at lunch."

Suddenly, Marcus is standing in front of me. He shoves his phone in my face.

"This you, Dress Code?" I look at the first photo Daniela and I so perfectly edited.

"Yeah."

"Huh." Marcus looks impressed. "You're planning a walkout?"

"Uh-huh. Tuesday after next, right before seventh period, after eighth-grade lunch. The assistant principals and counselors should still be in the cafeteria then."

"How many people you think are gonna go?"

Marcus hops on the desk across from me, scrolling on his phone. Does he want me to answer?

"1 don't know. That photo has one hundred and fourteen likes. And people have been sharing it in their Instagram stories, too. Maybe a hundred. Maybe more."

Marcus smiles. "And boys can do it, too?"

"Anybody who thinks the dress code is sexist."

"What about people who just want to see more girls in short skirts?"

If 1 were braver, 1 would roll my eyes. Marcus laughs. "I'm just kidding. You got to fight the good fight. We get that. You should've seen how tough it was to be on this team back when Mr. Eiger was the coach. It was all white kids." He turns to Sean, tousling his curls. "No offense, man."

"None taken."

Marcus sighs. "This school? It's not cool what they do to girls."

What *they* do? Apparently he doesn't realize that the Quiz Bowl boys aren't much better.

"We'll do it," Sean says, leaning so close 1 can smell the spice of his deodorant. "The whole team."

"We'll be like Mother Jones's 1903 March of the Mill Children," Marcus says.

"Or the Birmingham Children's Crusade," Sean adds.

"East LA Walkouts."

"Black Lives Matter."

"Parkland."

Leave it to Quiz Bowl kids to geek out over protests, though I wonder whether these boys willing to march for the dress code realize they're part of the problem.

chapter 17

The school parking lot is almost empty when our bus pulls up to Cactus Canyon Middle School on Saturday morning. It's our first Quiz Bowl match of the year, and even though it's not part of the official season, almost everyone's family is coming to watch. A few cars are already parked by the door. Most of the seats in our yellow school bus are empty since there's only thirteen of us huddled in the back. Mr. Shao sits right behind the driver, sipping coffee from a thermos. Thankfully, Daniela sat with me, though she paused before sitting down and her eyes flicked to Jamiya's seat three rows behind.

When the bus stops, Mr. Shao pops out of his seat, clutching his clipboard. "Don't leave any trash on the bus!" he calls, even though none of us needed a snack on the ten-minute ride. We gather our backpacks, people sending quick texts to their parents that we've arrived, and pile off the bus. I grab the buzzer system, one of my alternate jobs for the day. Jamiya makes everyone line up beside the bus for a picture for the team account.

As we walk toward the entrance, I spot Daniela's parents and her little brother, Miguel, waiting beneath the cement overhang. Mr. Jaimes waves Miguel's little hand at us, and Daniela rushes up to tickle his round belly. His giggles fill the empty parking lot.

"Hola, Margarita," Daniela's mom says as she kisses both my cheeks. "¡Buena suerte!"

No luck is needed to be the alternate, but I still thank her. Mr. Jaimes pulls Daniela into a side hug in one arm while Miguel wriggles in the other. He kisses the top of her head, and I reach over to squeeze Miguel's tiny foot in an adorably tiny sneaker.

"Is your dad coming, Margie?" Mr. Jaimes asks.

I shake my head. Dad still doesn't know I'm an alternate so he thought I was actually competing today, but for the millionth weekend in a row, he had too much work to leave his computer. He apologized all morning and even promised takeout. As the alternate, there wouldn't really be anything for him to see, but I'm still disappointed he's missing my first Quiz Bowl match of middle school. Hopefully he'll have more time next year when I actually make the team. If I make the team.

"We'll cheer for you both," Sra. Jaimes says, putting her arms around us. Her tasseled earring tickles my cheek, and I breathe in her spicy perfume. Even though she's not my mom, her hugs feel just as good. The door behind us clicks, and a kid in a red Cactus Canyon Quiz Bowl T-shirt opens the door. "We're in the library," he says, and everyone follows him through the dark hallways. Apparently they didn't turn the lights on for us.

As we walk, Daniela hands me a stack of note cards with questions. "Quiz me."

"Me too," Jamiya says, pulling out her earbuds.

I read the first card: "This opera, composed by Wolfgang Amadeus Mozart with a libretto by Lorenzo Da Ponte, explored the contentious relationship between social classes. The wedding plans of two servants—"

"Buzz, buzz, buzz," Jamiya says. "*The Marriage of Figaro.*"

"Fifteen points!" I say, flipping to the next card. Daniela gives Jamiya a high five.

"This Egyptian pharaoh oversaw the completion of many building projects, including two pairs of obelisks...obelisks at Karnak and a mortuary temple, Djeser-Djesru."

"How you doin', Margie?" Daniela laughs as I struggle.

"Fine!"

"Keep going!" Jamiya says, but Marcus stops us with a "Huddle up!" as we enter the library. Daniela hugs her parents goodbye before they go find seats. We all drop our backpacks in a large pile behind the nonfiction stacks.

"Hatshepsut," Jamiya whispers, and I check the card I'd already stuffed in my back pocket.

"Another fifteen points." She smiles.

"Phones off," Marcus says, and everyone pulls out their phones. "Off, not silenced. No mistakes."

Mr. Shao comes over. "You'll compete first against Cactus Canyon, and then we have a break before you play the other team."

"I thought it was only us and Cactus Canyon," Marcus says, and Mr. Shao shakes his head.

"A private school asked to participate so they're going to be here, too."

The Cactus Canyon team huddles in the corner. It's all boys. Every single one. I scan the library for the other team, but I only see one Hispanic boy standing with a woman I assume is his mom. He's wearing a blue shirt that I can't read from this far away. I wonder if his team is late.

"Here," Jamiya says, handing me a scrunchie with

an enormous blue bow. She hands one to Daniela, too. "My mom made these for us."

I quickly pull up my curls into a high ponytail. I love bows.

"Thanks," Daniela says, the bow still resting in her hand like a scorpion she doesn't dare startle. "But I don't do bows."

Jamiya smiles. "I thought maybe." She digs in her backpack and pulls out a button and hands it to Daniela. It has two brains, one with electricity buzzing all around it. It says "This is a brain. This is a brain on Quiz Bowl."

Daniela laughs. "This is awesome! Thank you!"

Mr. Shao and the Cactus Canyon coach go talk in the middle of the room, and Mikey calls out the A team for the first match: Marcus, Jamiya, Elman, and himself. I sit at one of the library tables near the action, ready to take notes: categories we struggle in, opponents' strengths and weaknesses. Knowing their strengths doesn't change the questions, but it's helpful to know where they're strong so we can beef up our knowledge. Be ready to hit the buzzer faster. In Quiz Bowl, sometimes that's all that matters. Daniela sits beside me studying a packet of questions while other kids read books. Xavier is secretly playing a video game on his phone under the table.

Cactus Canyon crushes us on the first three tossups, and I start an audit of which players get which questions correct. I quickly number the lines in my notebook so I can write the general theme for each question and then who got it right or wrong. As the questions fly, so do my fingers. Cactus Canyon beats us at almost every science question and most of the current events. We buzz in on the history ones, but they're faster. They miss one math question, but so do we. We do well on political science and sports. Marcus looks more and more frustrated as each question is read, and beneath the table Jamiya's right leg is bouncing at a hundred beats per minute. At the break, Daniela turns to me.

"We're getting destroyed."

"Annihilated."

"Crushed."

The moderator calls for the match to start again,

and the next nine minutes are painful as we only get five toss-ups and win only half the bonuses. Ugly. When the misery is finally over, our players flop to the floor in our corner, everyone muttering about how fast the Cactus Canyon team was and how their buzzers were probably rigged. I don't think it was the buzzers.

"Hey, hey, none of that," Mikey says, patting everyone on the back. "We have to own our losses if we want to own our wins. We have one more match left today. We can't be getting down on ourselves."

Our team is quiet as people pull out their phones, several people putting in earbuds while we wait. Sean passes around a bag of banana chips and some trail mix. I want to send a text to Dad, telling him how awful we're doing, but he probably wouldn't have time to respond. Finally, we're up again.

Marcus calls out, "Sean, Henry, José, Deven."

I turn to Daniela. "You're not playing this round? You should be! You were great at practice all week."

She shrugs, though I can see in her eyes she's disappointed. "The Kings pick teams."

"But you should definitely be on there. That's not

a balanced team because they're all math and science guys. They don't have anyone who's good at literature like you."

Daniela shrugs again, but she won't look at me. She presses a finger to the corner of her eye.

"Seriously! You should say something. They're underestimating you just because you're a girl!"

"You don't know that," Daniela snaps. "You're not the captain, so you don't know how they make decisions."

"But this feels unfair."

"Let it go, Margie. There's enough actual problems at our school without you seeing them when they aren't there. Quiz Bowl is the one thing I have to be excited about—please don't ruin it."

She marches toward the playing area, taking a seat next to Jamiya, who puts a hand on her shoulder. The two whisper together. Maybe that's what I should have done—just comforted my best friend.

The moderator steps up to the podium. "For this final round of our preseason match today, we have the Live Oak Middle School B team coached by Mr. Shao and Austin Day School coached by Ms. Almeida."

At the table across from our team sits the boy in the blue shirt. Alone. I elbow Xavier. "He's a team of one?"

He looks up from his hidden phone. "I guess so."

"We better not lose to one single kid."

He laughs. "Marcus and Mikey will destroy us in practice on Monday if that happens."

It happens.

He beats us by almost three hundred points. The matches are timed, so we couldn't just admit defeat after he got the first eighty-five points in a row. Instead, we spent the full eighteen minutes slapping at the buzzers and muttering answers seconds too late. I learned the boy's name is Mateo from the yelling of the adult fan club that showed up. It was eight times larger than his team.

"That kid is incredible," Daniela whispers as we trudge toward the bus. "Do you think he's really only in middle school?"

"He's not that tall," I whisper back, not wanting

anyone to hear us saying anything good about the boy genius. "But he is amazing."

"I'm going to sit with Jamiya on the ride back," Daniela says as she walks past me, taking a seat three rows behind.

I plop the buzzer kit in the empty seat beside me. Suddenly, I'm a team of one, too.

chapter 18

I'M COMFORTABLE WITH MY BODY, **BUT MY SCHOOL ISN'T.**

Daniela and I carry our lunch trays toward the library, where Jamiya is working as an aide. After we got destroyed on Saturday, we decided to start using our lunch as additional study time, and the librarian said that if Jamiya shelved all the books in the return bin, she could use the rest of her class period to study with us. With our first official match only ten days away, we have been studying every minute we can. Paper cuts line my fingertips from all the card flipping. Today we're supposed to focus on current events.

The library is empty when we get there except for Jamiya, who's checking in a stack of books. She's wearing an enormous Live Oak Middle School T-shirt.

"Give me a second to finish these last two," Jamiya says, holding up the bar codes to the scanner before adding the books to a cart behind her. Daniela and I set our lunch trays on one of the empty round tables.

When Jamiya walks around the counter with a stack of magazines in her arms, I realize the T-shirt goes halfway to her knees and billows at her sides like a ghost costume on Halloween.

"Is that—Did you get dress coded?" I ask, realizing her shirt might be the same as my terrible Live Oak shorts.

"Yep. Third period. Ms. Lohrstorfer's sub."

"I thought your parents didn't let that happen," I say as I open my chocolate milk.

"Oh, my mom is on her way." Jamiya drops into a chair beside us.

"I'm so sorry," Daniela says, and Jamiya shrugs.

"It's just annoying. And this shirt smells terrible." She lays the magazines out on the table between our trays.

"The gym shorts I had to wear smelled fine, but they looked disgusting."

"They're supposed to. It's our punishment for being female." Jamiya pulls at the sleeve of her T-shirt, which seems longer than the other, maybe stretched out in the wash.

"Do you want some?" Daniela asks Jamiya, offering her some cucumber slices from a ziplock bag. "I also have Skittles."

Jamiya shakes her head. "I'm fine. Thanks, though."

"If you don't mind me asking," I say, "what were you wearing that got you dress coded?"

Jamiya rolls her eyes. "I can show you."

She lifts up the enormous T-shirt to show a plain, white scoop neck top. The shirt is snug and the neckline is a little low, but it isn't especially revealing.

"You got dress coded for that?" Daniela asks. "Seriously?"

Jamiya drops the shirt down and shakes her head with exasperation.

"I'm really sorry," I say, reaching out to pat her shoulder. Jamiya flips open a copy of *People* magazine, the same one Grandma Colleen has on her nightstand. Daniela takes a bite of her lunch before grabbing a *Newsweek*.

Suddenly Jamiya looks at me. "I want to help with your protest. Like really help. What do you need?"

My mouth drops open. "Oh...Let me think."

Jamiya holds out a hand, and Daniela drops in some Skittles. "I'm up for anything."

I run through the list in my notebook. Gloria has social media pretty much taken care of now. "We do need posters?" I offer.

"Done," Jamiya says. "My mom would love to go on a shopping trip for supplies."

"You're going to tell your mom?" Daniela asks. I was thinking the same thing.

"Of course. My mom supports what I do, especially when it's speaking up for myself."

I bet Mom would have bought supplies with me. We would have stayed up late laughing and painting our posters, snacking on popcorn and preparing to fight. But I don't know what Dad would say if I told him. He'd probably want me to stay out of trouble. And he hasn't been around enough for me to even have the opportunity.

"Don't your parents know?" Jamiya asks, and even though I think she's asking both of us, I wait for Daniela to answer. She shakes her head. I didn't think she'd tell them. Her parents take getting in trouble very seriously, as if it's a reflection on her mom as a teacher and a parent. Daniela only got in trouble once in fourth grade, when the substitute teacher called home on us for talking too much, and she was grounded for a month.

"My dad doesn't know, either," I say.

Jamiya raises her eyebrows. "That's risky on a whole 'nother level."

I change the subject, not wanting to think about what will happen if Dad finds out I'm running a school-wide dress code protest. "So you'll make posters?"

"Sure. Easy. I'll get enough supplies to pass out to other girls who want to make them. What should I write?"

I give Jamiya the updates on the hashtags and Gloria's livestream. We agree to have her add a photo of the shirt she's wearing to the Instagram account tonight. Daniela silently eats her lunch.

"Are you sure this is the best way to do this?" Daniela finally says, twisting a button on her charcoal button-up. "Maybe we should have talked to the principal or something first?"

Jamiya shakes her head before I can answer. "My parents have talked to Mr. Franklin every year I've been here. He always says the same thing about school policy and keeping kids safe, as if my shirt is putting anyone in danger."

"What about Student Council? You could start a petition or something?"

"If he won't listen to parents, he's definitely not going to care about a petition signed by students."

"It's just...we could get in a lot of trouble," Daniela says. "Something way worse than having to wear an old T-shirt."

"Wearing an old T-shirt is pretty awful. You just don't know how bad it feels because you've never had to wear one," I snap, and Daniela frowns.

"That's because I would never wear something that would get me dress coded."

"So you think my skirt was inappropriate? That Ms. Scott was right?"

"No," Daniela argues, "I'm not saying—"

"Are you saying my shirt is distracting?" Jamiya asks, and Daniela's face falls. For a minute, I worry we're ganging up on her.

"No, that's not what I'm saying, I just—"

"You're right. You don't have to worry about it, because you're never going to get dress coded," I add. "You sort of dress like a boy, and boys don't get dress coded."

Daniela fumes. "Just because I don't wear skirts, doesn't mean I'm not a girl."

"I know," I say, softening. "I didn't mean it like that." Clothes have always been a struggle for Daniela since her family always wants her to dress more girly. Her closet is still crammed full of dresses from her abuela and her tías, even though she's told them a million times that's not who she is.

"I get the dress code is unfair," Daniela continues. "I just don't know if this is the right way to deal with it."

"Do you have any better ideas?" I ask.

"I told you—talk to Mr. Franklin."

"Jamiya already said that wouldn't work, so what else do you have?"

We stare at each other, like jousters ready to rush.

"Why don't we take a break from this dress code mess and focus on Quiz Bowl for a while since that's what we're supposed to be doing," Jamiya says, handing me a copy of *National Geographic*.

Daniela nods and begins flipping through the pages of a magazine, but I can tell she's not really memorizing any facts.

"I need you," I say, reaching for her hand. "I would still be taking grumpy audits in my little notebook without you."

Daniela laughs, but the breathy kind, the one she makes when she doesn't really think something is funny. She turns back to her magazine, and I wonder if she's going to turn her back on this protest...and on me.

chapter 19

HISTORY HAS ITS EYES ON YOU.

A knock at the door makes Ms. Anthony sigh from her spot at the whiteboard. So far this period we've already been interrupted by an office aide telling Jacob to leave early for his dentist appointment, a counselor to talk with Natalie, and another office aide to drop off a box Ms. Anthony smiled about but didn't open. She sets down her marker, weaving through the backpacks in our crammed seventh period. The person knocks again, louder this time.

"I'm coming," Ms. Anthony shouts.

When she opens the door, a scrawny eighth-grade boy with floppy black hair, sweatpants, and sandals with socks hands her a stack of papers. One earbud dangles around his neck, the other hidden beneath his hair. Ms. Anthony takes the stack from him, pausing to look at the pink sticky note on top, before telling him to put his electronics away. His sleepy eyes remain unchanged as he flicks the other earbud out of his ear and around his neck.

"Okay, so quickly, since we only have five minutes left," Ms. Anthony says, winding her way back to the board. She's reading the first paper and trips over Stella's backpack, catching herself on the back of a chair. "Oh! Okay. I'll hand these out at the end of class. Stella, don't let me forget."

I look down at my blank graphic organizer; I don't have room in my brain to compare the rights of women in matriarchal societies to women in modern America. I don't have time for a history lesson when tomorrow the girls at Live Oak are going to be making history.

Beep. Beep. Beep. The overhead intercom crackles.

"Seriously?" Ms. Anthony mutters. "How am I supposed to teach anything?"

"Good afternoon, Lions," Mr. Franklin says over the speaker. Normally Mr. Franklin starts all his announcements with a cringy "Wassup, scholars?" but this is different. Something's wrong. Everyone stops talking.

"This is your principal, Mr. Franklin," he continues. "It has come to my attention that some students are planning a walkout of class tomorrow because they are unhappy with some of the school rules. I encourage all students to come to my office to talk to me when they have concerns, but any students considering joining this walkout must know that the students planning this protest via social media"—he spits out the words as if he bit a poison dart frog— "did not give the proper notification to the school or acquire a permit, so this is not a legal protest. Students who choose to participate will receive consequences."

Thirty pairs of eyes shoot to me. I stare down at my notebook but glance up to see Ms. Anthony watching me with a strange look on her face.

The room is still as we wait. *What consequences?*

"These consequences include, but are not limited to, lunch detention, in-school suspension, and home-school suspension. The severity of actions could also lead to a removal to the alternative learning center." Someone gasps in the back of the room. "Thank you, Lions. Keep studying and make good choices."

I doodle on my paper, trying not to make eye contact with anyone, though I'm desperate to talk to Daniela, who is silent beside me.

"Well, then," Ms. Anthony says. "I guess that's what this letter is all about."

She walks through the tables, passing out the letter, her mouth opening, as if she's going to say something, but snapping closed before she does. She glances at the clock as she sets my letter down. Only three minutes until class ends.

The letter in my hands is so official. "Dear Live Oak Parent or Guardian," it reads, with the other side in Spanish. The letter says almost the exact same thing Mr. Franklin just told us, with an extra paragraph about monitoring their child on social media.

"We'll go ahead and get packed up for the day,"

Ms. Anthony says as she sets down the final paper. The room buzzes with whispers. Some kids sneak looks at their phones. Is someone going to show her the Instagram posts? The videos?

My whole body feels as if someone filled it with cement, my mass so heavy I wouldn't float, even in space. Carefully, I put my perfect-to-run-a-protest pencil in its case and shove my notebook in my backpack. Underneath the table, I text Gloria: **Did you hear the announcement?**

She responds with the person shrugging emoji and **Told you we'd get in trouble.**

You still want to do it?

She sends the 100 percent emoji and the winking face with the tongue out. I try to make eye contact with Daniela, but she's angrily shoving items into her backpack. My phone buzzes again. Gloria.

No te preocupes. It's gonna be great.

I wish I had half her confidence. What I really need is Daniela to talk to me, to make me feel relaxed. She helped me not freak out when I was wearing the terrible gym shorts. She told me to post the original photo. I need my best friend, but she's already at the front of Ms. Anthony's line. I move to the middle, cutting people behind me, but I don't want to be last, where Ms. Anthony could stop and ask me questions before I escape. She still looks at me every few seconds. Does she know it's me? She probably doesn't know. The account doesn't even have my name. But maybe. Sometimes teachers know everything.

The bell rings—taking the lid off a cannon—and kids burst out the door, the volume rocketing up in decibels. When I get outside, Daniela isn't waiting. Kids stare at me as they pass. I walk to eighth period alone.

Everyone is on their phones when I get to Mr. Shao's classroom after school. Even though we have our rematch with Cactus Canyon and the Wonder Boy School of One this weekend, no one is practicing question sets or researching topics. They're all buzzing about one thing: tomorrow's protest. Marcus, Mikey, and Sean are huddled in the back corner of the classroom. Mr. Shao is missing. Daniela sits next to Jamiya, who is tapping on her phone faster than the winds in a black hole.

"You ready to break the rules tomorrow?" Jamiya says with a smile as she sets her phone in her lap.

"Ready or not, here we come." I hope all my fake courage will churn up some real confidence. "We do have four hundred twenty seven followers now on Instagram since we posted your photo."

Jamiya nods. "Mr. Franklin's announcement got even more people fired up. Lots of kids were asking about it. I saw like twenty people had it on their phones."

"Good," I say, sitting down beside her, needing a minute to soak it all in. Daniela stares at the whiteboard as though it contains a lemon juice message she has to burn with her eyeballs to reveal. "Everyone knows the plan, so now we just wait."

"And you're really okay with getting in trouble?" Jamiya asks. "You were only in ISS one day, and it freaked you out so much you ran a school-wide protest."

"They can't really get us all in trouble, can they?

How would they suspend that many kids," I say, turning to Daniela. "Right?"

"Hey, everybody, huddle up!" Marcus calls before she can answer. We crowd into a tight circle, like a football team under the bright Friday night lights. The Kings stand side by side, a double commanding presence.

"You all heard Mr. Franklin today," Marcus says, his arms crossed over his chest. "Anyone who participates in tomorrow's protest could end up in lunch detention or even suspended."

"They're not really going to suspend all of us," Elman says. I'm glad to hear other people thinking the same as I am.

Marcus shakes his head. "We don't know what they'll do, but we do know this." He turns to Mikey, who reads from his phone.

"Any student receiving suspension, either in-school or homebound, is not permitted to participate in any district extracurricular activities, including but not limited to, sporting events, musical or theatrical performances, or academic competitions, during the duration of their suspension."

The room stills at "academic competitions." That's us. That's Quiz Bowl.

"This weekend is the first official competition, and we know what happened in the preseason meet. We got thrashed," Marcus continues, as everyone groans, remembering the pain of that loss. "For us eighth graders, this is our last chance to be champions. Our final opportunity to have a perfect season. We're not saying you can't walk out, but it's on you if you do. You have to decide your priority. Is it Quiz Bowl?"

He stares down each one of us, and every team member nods their head at his gaze. Everyone except Jamiya, who's watching with her eyebrows raised and her lips pursed.

"You girls know we got your back," Mikey says. "But we're not walking out. It's not worth the risk."

"Then how do you have our back?" Jamiya asks, stepping forward, out of the circle.

"We agree the dress code is unfair," Sean says, scratching his cheek. "We just can't risk getting suspended. Not after last time." The rest of the team nods, muttering about how stupid it would be to walk out. Someone even says the protest itself is stupid.

"So you'll only have our back when it's convenient?" Jamiya locks eyes with Mikey. "When it's easy?"

I step up beside her. "Just two weeks ago you said you would help us, and now this is a hundred eighty-degree turn. Protesting with us is the least you could do for the girls on this team, considering—"

"Considering what?" Marcus asks, looking down at me.

"Considering how you treat us."

The room breaks into shouts. Suddenly, the door pushes open, and Mr. Shao hurries in carrying a stack of copies and a half-eaten apple.

"You all better get practicing," Mr. Shao says, dropping the papers onto his desk. "Depending how tomorrow goes, Mr. Franklin might cancel all clubs for the rest of the week."

"What? No way!" the team shouts.

"So I'd stop wasting time with whatever you're doing and get those buzzers going."

Sean jumps up and grabs the box of buzzers even

though that's technically my job now. All the boys move to help him set up, or at least make themselves look busy. Marcus leans toward Jamiya and me. "You want to march, march. But you know the consequences." He turns and shouts, "Mikey, read the first matchup."

Mikey starts to call names for the first round of practice competition. I don't listen as I follow Daniela and Jamiya back to our seats.

"Got our back, yeah right," Jamiya mutters as she grabs her flash cards.

"You're still going to do it, right?" I ask.

"Yes," Jamiya says, surprised I even asked. "I knew what could happen; I'm not a flake."

Then I see it in Daniela's face. The crease in her forehead and the way her dark eyes keep sweeping past me, avoiding my eyes. She's looked like this before, once when she could only invite one friend to sleep over at her house for her birthday, and she picked her cousin instead of me. And another time when she chose to go to the coed Catholic summer camp when she was ten and I was still nine and only able to go to the girls-only camp. It's the look of betrayal.

"Daniela, you're still going to walk out tomorrow, right?"

She starts to shake her head no.

"Are you serious?"

"I'm sorry, Margie, but I can't."

"Are you worried because of what Mikey and Marcus said? Because I don't think they can actually suspend all of us for protesting. Not with this many people part of it."

"But we're not just part of it. We *planned* it."

"Which is why we have to be there!"

"I still support the protest. I'm just not going to march."

I scoff. "Marching *is* the protest. What are you going to do? Hold your poster up in the classroom where no one will see it?"

Jamiya puts a hand on Daniela's shoulder. "If you don't want to do it, that's fine. You don't have to explain; you just have to be sure of your decisions."

I ignore Jamiya. She might not need an explanation, but I do. "You knew we could get in trouble for this. It's not news. It's the first thing Gloria said when we asked her!"

"Yes," she argues, pretending to shuffle through her own flash cards. "We both knew what was going to happen. And if you're willing to get suspended and lose your chance of being on Quiz Bowl, that's up to you. You're the one who was so upset about getting dress coded in the first place, but you can't be mad that I'm not willing to get suspended over this."

"So it's okay if I get in trouble, but not you?"

"Yes," she says, looking over at Jamiya with a look I don't understand.

"What? Tell me!" I ask, furious that she's backing out when I need her the most.

"I'm sorry, Margie, but you heard Mr. Franklin and the Kings. We each have to decide what our priority is. You'll decide. Gloria will decide. Jamiya will decide. I've made my decision. I haven't worked this hard to get on the Quiz Bowl team just to get kicked off before our first match."

"But you don't even know if we'll get in trouble."

"I know *you* won't."

"I've already gotten in trouble for dress code," I argue. "I was suspended if you don't remember."

Jamiya watches our fight behind her flash cards.

"You were suspended once, but think about Gloria. Think about the other girls in ISS. Latina and Black girls get singled out and punished all the time. And I can't risk that. I've worked too hard to prove that I deserve to be on the team."

"Quiet in the back," Sean calls from the podium, and I pull Daniela's arm so we're sitting side by side.

"You can't quit now," I whisper, and she twists out of my grasp.

"Daniela!" Marcus calls. "Replace Xavier. He's got a bloody nose."

"Wait," I say, grabbing her arm, but she yanks away. She doesn't look back as she crosses to her seat at the table.

"Another person just sent me your post," Jamiya says, holding her phone out. I look at the name I don't recognize. Even with 427 followers I still feel alone when one of them isn't Daniela.

chapter 20

NOT FRAGILE
LIKE A FLOWER.
FRAGILE LIKE A
BOMB.

Grandma made stir-fry. "Stir-fry," with air quotes. The first time Grandma said she was making stir-fry, a few weeks after she moved in, I freaked out because I love all kinds of stir-fry: cashew chicken, crispy sesame beef, shrimp pad thai. I love the variety of vegetables, especially the snow peas, and all the spices. Dad says he's too lazy to make any stir-fry at home since he doesn't want to chop vegetables, but whenever we get Chinese takeout, it's what I order. Every time.

I should have been suspicious. I should have thought, hmm, how would my Irish grandma know how to make a stir-fry when she normally makes roast and cabbage and the most delicious soda bread. It wasn't stir-fry. It's still not stir-fry. Instead, Grandma has boiled vegetables in cream of mushroom soup. I spoon another bite of mush into my mouth. It doesn't taste bad; it's just not what I was expecting.

Like getting a cinnamon-flavored jelly bean when you thought it was cherry.

Like when you expect your best friend to have your back, and she picks Quiz Bowl over you.

Like stir-fry that is actually stew.

Across from me, Grandma eats in silence, occasionally pausing to jostle her dentures with her tongue. It doesn't gross me out anymore. Dad is sneaking glances at his phone because even though he's the one who set the no technology at dinner policy, he's the one always breaking it to answer work messages. Grandma huffs when she sees him, so he moves his phone to his lap like all the kids at school. He glances down between bites.

"I got a call from your school today, Margie-Moo," Dad says, his eyes back to me for the moment. "A robocall. What do you know about this protest?"

Stew glops off my spoon back into my bowl. He wouldn't be asking if they called and told him it was me. The account doesn't have my name anyway. Dad would recognize my skirt if he saw the post, but Mr. Franklin wouldn't. Unless someone turned me in. I wonder if Jamiya and Gloria are having this same conversation with their parents tonight.

"Margie?" Dad prods.

"What?"

"You mean, 'Beg your pardon,'" Grandma corrects.

"Beg your pardon?" I say, even though, *Oh my gosh, seriously, Grandma. Not now.*

"The call said some students are planning a protest at school tomorrow, and I'm supposed to advise you not to do it."

"Okay," I say, burying a mushroom beneath a pile of rice.

"It didn't say what they were protesting."

I shrug. "I heard it's about the dress code." He'll just keep pushing if I don't give him something.

"That seems like an odd thing to protest," Dad says as he taps on his phone.

"No, it's not."

Dad cocks his head. "Well, it's not like the Parkland kids protesting gun violence. And those were high schoolers. What do kids even want to wear that they can't already? Crop tops?"

I roll my eyes, as if the protest were just about wanting to show my belly button. Then Dad looks at me, really looks at me, the way he did the time I stole ten dollars off his nightstand so I could buy Girl Scout cookies. The X-raying-my-soul kind of stare.

"Dress code, huh?" he says, all fake breezy and casual. "You had a lot of feelings about the dress code."

I don't take the bait. "I'm fine."

"Hmm..."

"What's bad about the dress code?" Grandma interrupts, a spot of stew staining the embroidered collar of her blouse.

"It's sexist for one thing," I mutter, unable to stop myself.

"Aha! So you do have an opinion!" Dad slaps the table with both hands in triumph.

"Why doesn't the school have uniforms?" Grandma asks. "Nice slacks for the boys and skirts for the girls."

"Because skirts distract boys, according to the dress code, Grandma." The fire that's been fueling my engines all week begins to blaze. I stare right into Dad's eyes and give *him* the X-ray look this time.

"Margie," Dad says, leaning toward me. Do I tell him? I don't know. I can't trust that he won't try to stop me if I do. I don't know if he's 100 percent on my side like Jamiya's mom. Worst-case scenario, he could keep me home from school so I couldn't participate. "Is there something you want to tell me? Your principal said there would be serious consequences for anyone involved."

"Young girls shouldn't get in trouble," Grandma says, shaking her head.

Young girls are trouble.

"No," I say as I set my spoon in my bowl. "I know a protest is happening and that's it."

Dad raises an eyebrow. "This is your chance to be honest with me." His eyes drop to his phone for a millisecond, and now I definitely won't say anything. I'm not his priority anymore—his stupid job is. He wouldn't have time to listen to me anyway.

"May I be excused?" I ask, standing up and whisking my plate off the table before Dad has a chance to answer.

At nine o'clock, when I'm supposed to be falling asleep, I sneak my phone out of the kitchen so I can call Daniela. It's too late, and her parents won't be happy, but I have to talk to her. After four rings, her mom picks up.

"¿Bueno?"

"Buenas noches, Señora Jaimes," I say, ready to use the lie I already made up. "I'm sorry it's late, but can I talk to Daniela? It's a homework emergency."

Daniela's parents are serious about grades, way more than Dad is. He's all, "Do your best, and if your best isn't an A, that's okay!" Daniela's parents are "Do your best. Period."

"¿Una emergencia de tarea?" her mom asks, and then a long sentence in Spanish I don't understand.

"Por favor," I ask. "¿Un minuto?"

Because really, I only need a minute.

"Sí, pero no se demorren. It's very late." She must be really mad if she's using English with me. The phone goes quiet, the only sound the TV in the background as her mom passes through the house.

"Margie?" Daniela asks, and my breath sails out of my mouth.

"Are you sure you won't do it?" I whisper so Dad doesn't hear me.

Daniela sighs. "We already talked about this."

"I know, it's just..." I pause, looking across the room at the desk drawer where my homemade "Live Oak Code Breakers" shirt lies hidden beneath last year's Quiz Bowl study guides. "I don't think I can do this without you."

"I'll be at school tomorrow."

"You know it's not the same. I don't get it. Why won't you do it?"

"I can't, Margie."

"Please."

"If you thought about somebody other than yourself for a minute, Margie, you would know why I can't do it."

Her words punch like an atom bomb in my stomach, the radiation diffusing through my veins and scrambling my brains. Is there a truth everyone knows except me, like I'm the emperor standing naked in the street? Have I been missing it this whole time, a protective coating that shields me from trouble just because I'm white?

"Okay," I manage to whisper. "I'll see you tomorrow."

chapter 21

I'm roasting in my coral-red cardigan, each button closed, all the way up to the very top. This morning as I slurped my Frosted Flakes, Grandma Colleen said, "You look like such a classy young woman." She didn't know that below the sweater was a shirt that said "Code Breakers" in black Sharpie.

We only have a few minutes left in sixth period, and I try not to make eye contact with Mr. Kadura, who keeps staring at all the girls in the room, his wild eyebrows furrowing. Maybe he can sense what's about to happen with his teacher Spidey senses. Maybe the teachers already know.

Beside me, two girls dig in their backpacks, their hands patting the shirts they are hiding as they wait for the moment to change. Who knows how many people in this room have a T-shirt underneath their hoodie or stuffed into their backpack, just waiting for their superhero transformation? Somewhere in the eighth-grade building, Jamiya's posters hide between the folders and notebooks in her backpack like a stick of dynamite ready to explode. If we were at the airport, they would never let us through security with such flammable materials.

The seconds tick by, the moments counting down until this whole thing is out of my hands. Mr. Kadura rambles on about our upcoming web design project, and I avoid eye contact since I might start to smile or laugh because I'm nervous.

Then it happens. The bell rings, a sound so familiar and suddenly so life-changing. The students burst out Mr. Kadura's door, and I follow behind, slowly unbuttoning my sweater to reveal the homemade shirt. In the hallways, a smaller than usual amount of kids walk straight to their next class, their heads down as they plow through the anticipation filling the hall. Ten to twenty kids hover in the hallway. We should be going to our classes. We should be stopping at the water fountain. We should be lining up outside the classroom doors. The teachers are starting to notice something is wrong. They look at one another's doors, shaking their heads, their mouths forming words I don't have time to decipher. Mr. Kadura quickly types on his phone.

A group of girls rushes into the bathroom, their backpacks colliding as they try to squeeze in the blue metal door. I race in behind them, and someone offers me the open stall so I can change first. My jeans get stuck on my shoes, but I yank them off. The navy tulle is smooth underneath my fingers as I pull on the skirt that started it all. Once changed, I burst out the bathroom doors, charging through the crowded hallway toward the library, our meetup spot. The hallway is crammed with kids now, so many that I can barely squeeze past. The grades are starting to blend as we move toward the center of the school, a mix of boys and girls, diverse in every way.

I keep looking for Daniela even though she's in Ms. Anthony's class already, waiting for the commotion to start. I wonder how many kids will be waiting with her. Any? I scan the crowd for Gloria, knowing at least she'll be here to help lead the charge. I might have put the kindling on the fire, but she's the lighter fluid.

Suddenly Jamiya is by my side, sweat beading on her forehead. "I had to sprint to get over here," she says as she fans the bottom of her T-shirt. "Look at the turnout." The large crowd outside the library door churns, the energy buzzing as they wait for the signal. "Are you ready?"

I don't know. Maybe you're never ready when you're about to be brave. Maybe Amelia Earhart just got in the cockpit and started the engine, not worried about what would happen next. Rosa Parks sat down on the bus knowing she wasn't going to get up. Maybe you just do it anyway.

"Are you sure *you* want to do this?" I ask as some-one pushes me toward the library doors.

Jamiya laughs. "It's a little late now." She sets her backpack on the floor and pulls out a stack of post-ers. "Here," she says, handing a few to the kids in the crowd.

"I'm just asking because of what Daniela said yes-terday, about how I'm probably not going to get in trouble, but you guys are, you and Gloria, because—"

"Because I'm Black and Gloria's Latina?" Jamiya hands another poster to a boy wearing a homemade "Dress Code Sucks" T-shirt.

"Yeah..."

Jamiya smirks, passing out her last extra sign. "Of course that's true. That's not just a dress code thing."

Suddenly, Gloria's full voice shouts, "Hey, hey, ho, ho, this sexist dress code has got to go!" That was number two on the list of chants, but okay. Here we go!

"I'm just worried—"

"No time for that now, Margie," Jamiya says as

she hoists her poster above her head. "I make my own choices. Let's go!"

I unbutton the last button of my cardigan, ripping it off my shoulders and tying it around my waist, which looks tacky but there's no other place to put it. I really don't want to trample it; it's a nice sweater. Jamiya hands me a stack of posters to pass out. A ton of kids are already holding signs or screaming— maybe fifty, maybe a hundred—but maybe it only feels that way because we're all so close together in the hallway. Are more protesters somewhere else? I catch Gloria's eye, and she winks before descending the stairs.

"Hey, hey," I shout as I begin handing out Jamiya's posters to anyone who will take one. Someone pulls a poster out of my hand so hard that it cuts my palm. I ignore it, keeping the last poster for myself, and follow the group.

"We are not a distraction! We are not a distraction!" we chant, with the few boys beside me hollering, "I am not distracted!"

We turn down the hallway toward the science labs. "This is so awesome," someone shouts, then there's Xavier running up to me. He's made his own T-shirt with "I'm not distracted."

"You made a shirt?"

He nods. "My mom bought me some stuff at Walmart last night." I smile and cup my hands over my mouth as I chant.

After ten minutes my voice is hoarse from shouting, and my arms are bruised from being banged back and forth by students darting through the crowd as we march. I feel exactly like I do after a day spent at the beach: thrilled to have had the best day ever but also dried out, as if all my energy was left in the water. I raise my fist above the black-haired girl in front of me and part of me thinks, *I wish I had a Popsicle right now.* And equality.

We turn the corner near the main office, and all the secretaries stare at us through the windows, the phones pressed to their ears momentarily forgotten. Teachers are stationed alongside the walls as we march. Mr. Shao leans against the stairs as if he's watching golf or some other incredibly boring sport. He doesn't seem to realize what's happening. We're taking over the school right now, and I think I saw him yawn.

Beep. Beep. Beep. The intercom bursts into sound, and even though we keep marching and some kids keep cheering, we all sense it. A girl beside me screams, "I am not a distraction" right in my ear, and I want to tell her "shh," so I can hear the announcement, but I don't.

"Live Oak students. This is your principal, Mr. Franklin. It is time for all students to return to their classes. I repeat, all students must return to their classes. Students who do not immediately return to their classes will receive disciplinary consequences. Teachers and staff, please help escort students to their assigned rooms."

A few students—the ones like me, who usually follow the rules and never get in trouble—start looking at the adults on the sidelines. But we don't stop. We don't follow the rules today. We keep marching. We keep shouting, and it feels the same as it did when I was with Dad at the Women's March, all those women and all those people on the streets. It's different this time since I'm not doing it because someone else told me to. I'm not just the cute kid to take a picture of as a hoped-for future leader. We are the leaders. Now. Today. Not in the future. Not in twenty years. We, the girls of Live Oak Middle School, are changing our world. One dress code policy at a time.

I wish my mom could see me. I know she would be proud.

"Okay, okay, let's go. You heard Principal Franklin," a teacher in a purple dress shouts as she claps her hands at us. The crowd ignores her, even as other teachers push closer to us from the edge of the hallways, like the squeezing walls in one of Dad's old adventure movies. My heart is still pounding, the chants fresh on my lips, but I can feel the tug of exhaustion creeping in.

"I am not a distraction!" I shout, and when a classroom door beside us opens, a few kids go in. Up ahead, one of the assistant principals, Mr. Vargas, barks into a headset.

"I am not a distraction!" I shout again, looking down at my T-shirt to give myself an extra dose of courage. I'm not ready to be finished.

Beep. Beep. Beep. The intercom again. Mr. Franklin: "All students must be in a classroom in the next two minutes or they will receive in-school suspension for disruption and insubordination. Teachers, please escort students to the nearest classroom, even if it is not their assigned room."

Mr. Vargas steps forward. He's so close that I can see the tiny basketballs embroidered on his tie. Most people have stopped chanting now, and we're beginning to disperse, like dandelion seeds blown from the stem. All around me kids are turning and walking in opposite directions. I've lost Jamiya in the crowd, but she should be heading to the eighth-grade building anyway.

"You have one minute," Mr. Vargas calls, and the other teachers stationed in the hall repeat him like an echo in a cavern. "One minute!"

I guess it's done, though it feels strange to just walk back to class. Regardless, I have a long way to go to get to Ms. Anthony's room so I start walking faster, suddenly more afraid, but also excited—a true solution, not a mixture, where you can't tell the different emotions apart. The hallways are almost empty now, but I still have half a hallway and a set of stairs to go.

Beep. Beep. Beep. "All students still in the hallway will be escorted to in-school suspension to be processed. Available teachers and staff, please escort all students to the in-school suspension room now."

I decide to run. Yes, I've been in ISS before, but for stupid dress code, not for "disruption" and "insubordination"! My shoes clatter as I sprint down the hall. I can see the bottom of the staircase, the portal to freedom, and then—

Ms. Scott is waiting with her hands on her hips, her bun even higher on her head. "Have you enjoyed your little adventure?" she asks with the terrifying smile of the villain in every movie ever.

"I'm going to class."

"You heard Mr. Franklin's announcement. All students still in the hallway must be escorted to ISS."

Down the hall I can hear someone arguing with an adult, shouting and scuffling. Even Ms. Scott looks, and there she is, Gloria, wearing jean shorts and her own homemade T-shirt. It's tied up in a knot on the side, and a glimpse of her stomach shows when she lifts her arms.

"I know! I'm going! You don't have to keep telling me," Gloria says, shrugging off the three adults following her down the hall. We watch the group turn the corner, and a weight drops into my stomach. I wonder how many other kids didn't make it to their classrooms and are now getting escorted to ISS, where Ms. Padilla waits to call their families.

Ms. Scott smirks. "Actions have consequences."

I await my punishment, knowing freedom is only a flight of stairs away. Daniela is safe in Ms. Anthony's classroom. I wonder what she knows already. What she's heard. Has she seen any of the posts on someone else's phone?

Ms. Scott assesses me, her arms folded tight across her chest.

"I suggest you get to class as fast as possible."

"Thank you!" I say before realizing Daniela was right. My stomach clenches. I'm not getting in trouble, but Gloria is. Just as I reach the first set of stairs, Ms. Scott stops me, her eyes gesturing to my Live Oak Code Breakers shirt.

"I suggest you put on that sweater. Your demonstration is over."

She smiles one more time, a smile that makes me wish for spinach in her teeth. I run up the stairs, not waiting for her to change her mind.

chapter 22

Ms. Anthony is showing a documentary about women in the media, but no one is watching. Not even her. I doubt anyone is trying to teach after the protest. We only have ten minutes left in the class period anyway. Ms. Anthony tries to keep us off our phones, moving to squash any screen that lights up the dark classroom, but it's too late. The videos are already posted on Instagram and YouTube, probably even Bubble. I'm grateful for the quiet since I can't imagine answering discussion questions when my heart is still pounding this fast.

Daniela hasn't said a word to me since I slunk back into Ms. Anthony's room. I keep waiting for her to ask a question or reach over and squeeze my hand, but she's staring at the screen as if it's the most important thing in her life.

"Do you know if Jamiya...," I ask in a whisper, roasting now under my cardigan, which is back on but still unbuttoned. "She hasn't responded to my text."

Daniela shakes her head, not even looking my way.

"I think Gloria might have gotten in trouble."

That spins her around. "Told you that was gonna happen."

I button my sweater, getting the buttons mismatched at first. "I don't know for sure."

Daniela shrugs, her eyes back on the screen.

"Ms. Scott stopped me on my way up here, but she let me go."

"Different girls. Different consequences," Daniela says with a look like I'm a fifth grader again, someone who doesn't know the basics of life.

"But lots of kids participated."

"Great."

"Can you stop doing that?"

"Stop doing what?"

I can feel the fire moving to my cheeks. "Stop being a jerk. You're the one who didn't want to be a part of the protest, and now you can't say anything nice about the fact that we just ran a huge school-wide walkout to change the dress code?"

"What do you want, Margie? Balloons?"

"You're just mad that you were too scared to participate. The protest was amazing and you missed it. You said it was Quiz Bowl, but we both know the Kings aren't going to let you play. They don't need you."

Her mouth drops open, and I wish I could pull the words back, but they're already speeding away like the rapidly expanding universe.

"I'm sorry—"

"Don't bother." Daniela turns in her chair, and even though she's close enough that I can smell her lavender laundry detergent, my best friend couldn't feel farther away.

The Kings might not need Daniela, but I do.

Where are you? I text as I run across the street, certain I'm going to crash into a kid or a car with my eyes glued to the screen. With all after school activities canceled—including Quiz Bowl—I only have a few minutes before the buses leave, but I have to see Gloria before I head home. My backpack pounds against my body as I jump the curb and race toward the 7-Eleven. I check my phone as I pull open the doors, jumping back to get out of the way of three eighth-grade boys carrying out an armload of soda and chips.

7-11, Gloria finally texts back. I roll my eyes. I knew that.

I'm in the middle of writing "where" when she calls my name. Gloria waves me over to the cooler.

"Are you okay?" I ask. "I saw you with those teachers. Did you get suspended?"

Gloria smirks as she holds up her fingers. "Three days."

"No! I'm so sorry!"

"I'm not," she says, grabbing a soda. "I've gotten in trouble at this school enough times for no reason, por estar parada allí no más, so at least this time it was for something real. Do you want one?"

"Gracias," I say, and she grabs another bottle. She hands it to me and opens hers, taking a huge drink.

"Are your parents going to be mad?" I ask, still not sure whether I'll tell Dad. Since Ms. Scott let me go, I have the luxury of not having to tell him.

"My mom has bigger things to worry about right now," Gloria says. "She's not going to be happy, but honestly, vale la pena. We finally got to say something about the way this school treats us."

She pauses. "Did you get caught? I saw you with that teacher."

Shame floods my veins. "No, she let me go."

"Como la Rosa de Guadalupe, tienes suerte." I'm not sure Daniela would call it luck. She doesn't look upset, not like Daniela, but I can feel my cheeks burning again. Gloria grabs me around the shoulder, laughing. "Cálmate, chica, that's a good thing. Now you don't have to spend the day in stupid ISS."

"Do you know anyone else who got suspended?

I haven't heard from Jamiya." I follow Gloria to the checkout. She drums her fingers on her soda bottle.

"I didn't see her. There were a couple kids, mostly girls, but I don't know how many of them will get actual referrals. Some kids just got talked to and sent back to class."

"Really? But not you?"

"I ran my mouth, so como te dije..." Gloria splays her hands as if three days of suspension were the logical conclusion.

"This school is so unfair."

"But maybe that's changing." Gloria sets her soda on the counter. "I got yours. Don't you have to catch the bus?"

I look out the window to see the first bus pulling out of the driveway.

"Yeah, I should go," I say, and she shoves my soda at me, laughing.

"We did it, Margie," she calls as I race toward the door. "¡Disfrútalo!"

chapter 23

Dad is washing windows when I get home. At four o'clock on a Tuesday, he is not in his fancy downtown office, but here. Cleaning. This cannot be good.

"You're home early," he says as he spritzes the glass panes in the dining room.

I could say the same about you.

"Clubs were canceled."

"Right. For the protest. I got another automated message from your school about the walkout."

I slink past him toward the kitchen and hear his footsteps behind me. I yank on the fridge door and look at all the Tupperware containers full of leftovers and no good snacks. I open and close the veggie drawer looking for something other than an onion and finally settle on some blueberry yogurt. Dad moves around me, spraying the window above our sink, whistling while he dries it with a paper towel. He never whistles.

"Dad," I complain, and he shrugs. "You know what you're doing."

"I'm just taking advantage of my early afternoon to wash some windows."

"You didn't leave work to clean house. You came home early because you knew there were no after school clubs," I say as I take a seat at the counter.

"And there was a school-wide protest that my daughter had something to do with."

I freeze, my heart launching into my throat. "Who told you?"

Dad eyes me across the counter. "You told me. Just now."

I should have kept my mouth shut. Though, honestly, I feel the tiniest bit relieved.

"I know you didn't get in trouble, because I didn't get *that* call," Dad continues. "All the parents are talking about it in the Facebook group."

"You guys need to get a life."

"Don't talk to your father that way," Grandma Colleen says as she comes out of her room with a laundry basket tucked under her arm. She starts tossing whites into the washer.

"Hate to break it to you, Margie, but you are my life," Dad says as he sprays the counter. "It's in my dad job description. So?"

"So, what?"

"Margie." The tone tells me I better knock it off.

"Fine. I started the protest. It was my idea, and then some other girls and I planned it. We shared it on social media. We marched in the hallways, and now it's done."

"Oh, Margie!" Dad says, his fingers massaging

his forehead. "I don't know whether to yell at you or applaud you. This is a big deal. Your principal robocalled the entire school twice. How did you even do this?"

"It doesn't matter," I say, jamming my spoon in my yogurt. "We had to do it. The dress code is sexist, Dad! Only the girls ever get dress coded. And if you do, you might spend hours doing nothing in ISS or they make us wear these enormous, gross gym shorts to embarrass us—"

"Wait. When did you have to wear gym shorts?"

"On the first day of school!"

"You didn't tell me that."

"Well, I had enough going on with not getting into Quiz Bowl—"

"You're not on the Quiz Bowl team? You've been going to practice."

"I'm just an alternate!"

"Wow, Margie, this is a lot of information. And a lot of lies."

I pound my hand on the table. "I didn't lie. I just didn't tell you. Because I didn't need you! I'm in sixth grade now! And you're too busy with work to care anyway!"

"Don't yell at your father," Grandma calls from the washer.

"I'm not yelling. I'm just being loud!"

"Whoa, whoa, whoa, everyone take a deep breath." Dad presses his palms on the counter, his head dropping behind him. "Your mother told me raising a teenage girl was going to be hard, and you're not even a teenager yet."

"I'm eleven. That's double digits."

He laughs, shaking his head and raising his hands in disbelief.

"That's right, Marge. Let's take a minute here to go back to the beginning."

I tell him the whole story, from the moment Ms. Scott's ruler rested against my bare leg to the gym shorts to Dress Code to the boys never getting in trouble and Gloria and all the girls stuck in suspension. Even Grandma Colleen listens to me without interrupting.

"Ms. Scott really said that your skirt was a

distraction?" Dad asks, his hands pressed to his temples. "And she measured you in class, in front of all the other kids? I am going up to school tomorrow to talk to your principal. This is not okay."

"No, Dad! We handled it."

"We'll see about that," he says, reaching out a hand to pat mine. "You're not in trouble for running this protest, but you are going to be homebound for the next few weeks."

"You mean I'm grounded? For marching?"

Dad shakes his head. "No. There's nothing wrong with you using your voice. Honestly, your mom would be proud. But you lied to me—about the skirt, about Quiz Bowl, about a school-wide walkout you orchestrated—"

"But you haven't really been around much to tell you anything. And when you are here, you're always on your phone or your computer."

Dad pauses, running a hand across his chin. "You're right. This new job has been tough on all of us." He looks over at Grandma, who's sorting clothes. "I'll make some changes so we can spend some needed time together. Maybe Grandma and I can help you practice your question sets. Get you ready for the team next year."

"Grandma does know a lot about celebrities."

Grandma smiles. "I know a lot more than that."

The door pushes open as I lay on top of my comforter, and I expect it to be Dad coming to tell me to turn the light off and go to sleep. My bedtime was almost an hour ago, but I can't do anything but lie here looking up at the stars, wondering how everything could feel so great and so terrible at the same time.

Grandma Colleen pokes her head around the door. "Margaret," she calls, and I prop myself up on my elbows.

"Yes, Grandma?"

Her wrinkled fingers curl around the door. "You're still awake?" I nod. "Do you want me to make you some chamomile tea?"

I shake my head. Tea can't solve my problems.

"Did you need something, Grandma?" I ask, and she shakes her head before coming to sit on the edge of my bed. She pulls at the collar of her nightgown. She bought me a similar one when she moved in, and honestly, I love it, but Teravista is usually too hot for a full-length nightgown. Grandma reaches out to cover my hand with hers.

"When I was your age, my best friend, Mary Catherine, and I wanted to be altar girls. My older brother, Tom, was an altar boy, and he got to wear the white robes and help the priest each Sunday. I wanted that job."

I sit up a little more as Grandma continues.

"Mary Catherine and I asked Father Michael if we could be altar girls. It wasn't that different than setting up a supper table or cleaning up the dishes. We could carry the chalice. We could pour the water to wash his hands."

"Did he let you?" I ask, thinking about how I refused to be an altar girl, even though Daniela and I went through the training. I was too embarrassed to stand up in front of the whole church in those stuffy white robes.

"No," Grandma says, patting my hand before interlacing her wrinkled fingers with mine.

"Really? Why?"

"He said that altar serving was a preparation for the priesthood, and of course, girls could not be priests."

"They let girls do it now."

Grandma sighs. "Things are different for you. Back then, I could only watch Tom, then Peter, then Michael, then John all serve while I sat in the pew with my mother." She smiles. "Mary Catherine and I did once sneak into the sacristy to try on the altar server vestments, but we were found out when we both told Father Michael in confession."

She laughs, and I do, too, surprised at my grandmother breaking any rule, especially a rule at church.

"I don't know much about your dress code and your protest, but..."

Grandma brushes back one of my curls.

"You're a very brave girl, Margaret. Maybe you and your girlfriends will get what you want."

I hope we can. For me, for Gloria and Jamiya, for Daniela, for all the people at Live Oak who want the freedom to be who they want and wear whatever they choose, and even for Grandma Colleen, who didn't want to wear a sequined, tulle skirt, but a long white robe. Different girls, different clothes, same goal. I only hope I'm still brave enough to help make it happen.

chapter 24

The next day at lunch, I linger by Ms. Anthony's door on the way the cafeteria. It's not like Daniela will be waiting to sit with me anyway. Ms. Anthony stands on a chair, digging through a pile of handmade posters on the top of her gray filing cabinet. Her multicolored skirt sways as she yanks at the poster board.

"Do you need help?" I ask, noticing an unopened

Tupperware container of salad sitting on Ms. Anthony's desk.

"Aren't you headed to lunch?" she asks, looking down at my lunch box.

"I'm not really that hungry."

"Well then, sure, Margie, thanks." She hands me a poster on the types of political systems and another on ancient civilizations of Mesopotamia. A few dust bunnies float down and land on my shoulders.

"I really need to get these organized one year." Ms. Anthony sighs. She gives one final yank, her ballet flats slipping on the chair before she catches herself on the side of the nearby window frame. "Got it!"

She hands me a large white poster with cartoon pictures of a TV, magazine, computer, and cell phone, and the title "Who is telling the story? Whose story is missing?" I set it down on a desk before handing her up the extras.

"I really like your class," I say as she shoves the posters back onto the cabinet. "Especially this unit, about women and society."

Ms. Anthony smiles, her magenta lipstick popping against her deep-brown skin. She rubs her hands along her skirt before climbing down.

"Me too. That's why I start the year with it. It's one of my favorites."

I pause, knowing what I want to ask her. No one said the words out loud today—"dress code," "protest," "walkout"—but the school buzzed, a slow hum like a beehive, the energy filling us all up, the teachers and principals waiting for us to sting. Each time I saw an empty seat I wondered: Suspended or home sick? Suspended or a field trip? Jamiya hasn't responded to a single text, but Gloria sent me a few before she started her first day of in-school suspension. All day I've been wondering what other girls are sitting there with her, boredom filling up their brains instead of knowledge. I know what those girls look like, and I still feel guilty that it isn't me.

Hoping I know what she'll say, but worried about her answer since she is a teacher after all, I finally ask: "What did you think of the protest?"

Ms. Anthony raises an eyebrow. "I'm still sorting that out. What did you think?"

"I *thought* it was a good thing."

"Thought?"

I trail my fingers along the edge of a desk. "My mom was an activist. She used to go to a lot of marches and protests."

Ms. Anthony takes the poster to the empty bulletin board. A dark rectangle waits in the center of the green paper, the outside edges faded by the sun.

"Does she march much anymore?" Ms. Anthony asks, smoothing out the curled edges of the poster with her palm.

"She died of cancer before I was two."

"Sorry to hear that, Margie."

"But my dad still takes me to marches sometimes. Well, only one so far. We went to the Women's March last year. Did you go?"

Ms. Anthony holds the poster up on the board. "I did not."

"Really? Why not?" Ms. Anthony is the exact type of person I thought would be at the Women's March. We've been talking about women's rights in her class since the very first week of school.

"Hand me those, please," Ms. Anthony says,

gesturing toward a container of pushpins. I move closer so I can hold the box for her. "I didn't attend because while I agreed with a lot of the march's focus on women's rights, I felt the organizers and many of the attendees disregarded the issues specifically affecting Black women and other women of color."

"Oh." I feel another rush of guilt into my stomach.

"I also had concerns about representation for the LGBT community. While well-intentioned, the march wasn't as intersectional as it needed to be. We can't march for women's rights without considering the different identities women have and the way those identities affect how they are viewed and treated by society." Ms. Anthony steps back to look at her poster. "That corner is crooked, isn't it?"

I nod, and she takes out the pin so she can line up the edge with the other side.

"So, about the protest yesterday?" she continues. "I need more information to decide if it was a protest I would have wanted to join. What was the organizers' motivation? What students were represented? Were the dress code challenges for girls of color or queer girls or nonbinary people considered and vocalized?"

My chest tightens. "No...I mean sort of...but no."

A tear slinks down my cheek. *How did I get this so wrong?* Ms. Anthony smiles.

"This was your, what, second protest march?"

I nod.

"That's why I'm teaching these concepts to you: sexism, racism, the importance of recognizing the intersectionality of our identities, that place where all these important parts of who we are mesh together with purpose. The march you girls led might create some really good change for the school. It might not. But now that you know better, you can do better."

Know better. Do better.

That seems like something I can handle. A fresh start. Maybe Daniela and I can have a new beginning to our friendship, too.

I sniffle, and Ms. Anthony hands me a tissue.

"My last one," she says, tossing the empty box into the blue recycling bin. "Thankfully, we're fully stocked at the beginning of the school year." She opens a closet to reveal boxes and boxes of Kleenex and hand sanitizer.

"You've got a lot of passion, Margie, so keep asking questions. Learn to use your voice in a way that your message becomes a harmony, not a solo."

I smile, thinking back to our voices chanting in the hallway. Gloria, Jamiya, me, and the other students of Live Oak. Many voices, but one song.

"You're late, Dress Code!" Marcus yells as I fly into the room, my backpack sliding back and forth behind me. "Hope you're ready 'cause you're up."

"What?" I ask as I look at the two rows of faces already set up for our practice round. Saturday is the big meet. All familiar faces in the seats except...no Jamiya. And no Daniela. *What's happening?*

"You're in, Dress Code. Elman's got strep throat, and Jamiya's suspended so she can't compete."

No! That must be why she hasn't responded to any of my texts. Or maybe she's mad at me for getting suspended. This can't be happening. She has to compete. "But we need her!"

Mikey shrugs. "It's not right, but she knew the consequences before she decided to march."

I cringe. "And Daniela?"

"She's getting copies of the new practice set from the library printer."

Mr. Shao's head peeks around the mountain of junk on his desk. His own Mount Shao. I smell tacos. And maybe cotton candy. Just then Daniela comes through the door, her breathing heavy as she holds a stack of copy paper.

"Got 'em!" she says before glancing at me. "Did they tell you you're on the team now? Congratulations." Her words sting like bare feet covered with fire ants. Neither of us wants me to be on the team this way.

"Let's go, people," Marcus says, tapping his fist on the table. He stands up, pulling on the hem of his black T-shirt. "We're down one practice because of yesterday's protest."

Sean pats the chair next to him. "You're on our team."

"Jamiya's our person for world religions, chemistry lab techniques, civil rights leaders, and general music and dance," Marcus says. "You good with any of those?"

"Some," I say, though I know nothing about chemistry lab techniques and only minimal facts about world religions and dance. Daniela and I got extra books from our librarian during Black History Month last year so I know more than the basics on civil rights leaders. I know about Claudette Colvin and Malcom X, but there is no way I compare to Jamiya. She said she didn't need Quiz Bowl to learn about her history. She's been drilling all her topics for months, probably for years, refining her expertise. She has two extra years of knowledge. She should be here. She should be competing Saturday.

I know what I need to do.

Phones are ringing nonstop in the front office, and the two secretaries run back and forth between the phones and the parents waiting in line. I've never seen so many parents in the office, not even on registration day. The secretaries switch between English and Spanish, their smiles big, too big for how tired their eyes are. I get in line behind a large woman with kaleidoscope leggings and a hot-pink top. She taps her toes while she waits, her neon-green toenails flashing in the peep toe of her shoe. I take a deep breath, imagining all the items that have given me strength: my skirt, my homemade protest shirt, the Saint Joan of Arc pendant sitting at home in my jewelry box.

Right now, I don't have anything to give me strength, but me.

When it's finally my turn, I step up to the counter. "I need to speak with Mr. Franklin, please."

"What about?" the secretary asks, twisting the charm bracelet around her wrist.

"I need to talk to him about the protest." She raises an eyebrow before gesturing to the people standing and sitting outside Mr. Franklin's office.

"Join the line."

I find an open space next to the fire extinguisher. At least six adults are waiting. No kids except me. I slide down the wall, sitting on the floor with my legs scrunched up in front of me. I pull out a stack of Quiz Bowl cards to study while I wait. I'm sure

Marcus and Mikey are furious that I left in the middle of practice, especially when I was already late, but I couldn't help it. I have to tell Mr. Franklin that the protest was my idea. None of these girls would be in trouble if it weren't for me.

I read one card: "This religion that contains 15.1 percent of the world's believers does not have a single founder or founding incident." Taoism? Hinduism? I toss the card back in the pile without bothering to look at the answer. Jamiya would have known. She knows world religions. My answers will never be more than a guess. I need to get in that office.

For forty-five minutes I wait on the floor until finally Mr. Franklin's "Who's next?" means me. His face tells me that he doesn't want to have another conversation and definitely not with a kid.

"Me!" I hop off the floor, brushing the dust bunnies off my shorts.

I sit down in front of Mr. Franklin's desk. The room is decorated like the inside of a craft store. There are several motivational signs painted on wood and a large rectangular mirror with a twisted iron frame. His desk is empty except for a neat stack of papers and a few picture frames, but I can only see their black velvet stands.

Mr. Franklin takes a deep breath. "What can I do for you, Ms....?"

"Kelly. Margaret Kelly. I'm in sixth grade here."

Obviously. Why would I be talking to the principal if I didn't even go to school here? This is not starting off how I planned, but I refuse to let it be another Ms. Scott conversation. I pull my sweaty legs off the fake leather seat and scoot forward in the chair so my feet are firmly on the ground. I press my hands on my thighs like I do before they ask a question in Quiz Bowl. My ready position.

"Mr. Franklin," I say, the words catching in my throat. "I planned the protest yesterday. It was my original idea because I was dress coded on my first day of school."

Mr. Franklin lifts his bushy eyebrows, rubbing a hand against his white-speckled stubble. It's strange to see his face at the same time I hear his voice. Normally, it's one or the other: I see him standing in the corner of the lunchroom or hear his voice over the intercom.

He tilts his head as if waiting for me to keep going.

"I will accept any punishment I have to take, but that's not really why I'm here. I'm here because some girls got in trouble for being involved, and they shouldn't be in ISS if I'm not." I feel tears welling in my eyes. "Or they shouldn't be at all. For example, Jamiya? She's an eighth grader in Quiz Bowl, and she can't participate in our big meet against Cactus Canyon, but we need her. Yes, she participated in the protest, but so did like half the school."

Mr. Franklin rolls his eyes as though he vividly remembers hundreds of kids marching in his halls.

"She participated in the protest, but that's part of our rights as students. I think."

Mr. Franklin leans back in his chair. "Let me ask you a question, Margaret: What is it you're wanting from me?"

Of all the things he could possibly change at this school, right now I only want one thing.

"I don't think any students should get in trouble for the protest."

"Skipping class, even for a protest, is against

school rules. And an unplanned walkout created an unsafe environment."

"But not all girls who marched got punished. Just some girls. And that's not fair."

"I can't share the disciplinary actions for individual students," Mr. Franklin says. "But you don't need to worry about the Quiz Bowl team. Ms. Dawson's parents were in earlier and...made a case."

I smile, relief fueling me. "That's great. Thank you. But what about the other girls in ISS?"

Mr. Franklin rolls his shoulders, sending a crackle down his spine.

"Again, I can't describe specifics about the school's disciplinary decisions—"

"You don't have to tell me what happened," I argue. "I know what happened. Not all girls got in trouble. Ms. Scott let me go free while my friend Gloria got three days' suspension. Why did she get in trouble when I didn't?"

"We strive to treat all students fairly," Mr. Franklin says, his mustache scrunched near his nose.

"But you didn't!"

Mr. Franklin looks at me and I wonder what he

sees. Does he see a girl who never breaks the rules? A girl who always does the right thing? A girl who's polite? A girl no one thinks is dangerous? Is my skin color the reason he believes all those things?

"I'm wondering if maybe the reason I didn't get in trouble when Gloria did was because I'm white, and she's Latina."

Mr. Franklin swallows, his eyebrows furrowed.

"That's a big accusation to make, and something the school will definitely look into. But for future concerns, I ask that you join Student Council. I meet with them once a semester. That's why students get eight hall passes per grading period now, instead of six."

"Maybe, but I can't wait for elections. We need to make changes now."

"You can always submit a suggestion to the box in the front office. I review those weekly."

Mr. Franklin glances over at the clock on his computer.

"How about now?" I say, feeling the same surge of confidence I felt yesterday as we marched through the halls.

"We can start," Mr. Franklin says with a slight sigh. "You're my last one of the night anyway."

"And could you also have a meeting for other girls to speak up? Like at lunch? I'm here now, but this doesn't just affect me."

Mr. Franklin sinks back in his chair. "We probably can work that out. For now, why don't you start from the beginning?"

I reach for my courage, realizing it was closer to the surface than I expected it to be. I'm more confident now than I was that first day of school. I press my hands down into Quiz Bowl ready position.

"Did you know that our dress code unfairly targets girls, especially girls of color, labeling us a distraction? On my first day here, I wore this skirt...."

chapter 25

**YOU.
ME.
THEM.
ALL OF US.**

The next day I race to practice so I can meet Daniela before it starts. She wouldn't talk to me all day: she ignored my glances in Ms. Scott's class and picked a new seat in Ms. Anthony's. I couldn't even find her at lunch. Now, I wait beside the door, welcoming the team like Grandma and I do when she signs us up to be greeters at mass. "Hello, hi," I say with a nod, and mostly the boys just walk by looking confused, but Mikey does nod and call me Dress Code as he passes.

Finally, I spot Daniela on the stairs with Jamiya. Their heads are tilted together as if they're sharing a secret, and I ignore the pang in my chest. Jamiya checks her phone and winks at me. She already knows what I'm about to do. She finally called me last night after she got her phone back. It was confiscated during the protest, but in the meeting with Mr. Franklin, her parents demanded its return. We talked for over an hour last night, and I told her everything that happened with Daniela, my ignorance and her silence. Jamiya even shared about the fights she's had with her best friend, who's in high school now. Jamiya gives me a look as she walks into the room, leaving Daniela by herself.

"Daniela, can we talk?" I say, stepping in front of the door.

"Practice starts in five minutes."

"I'll be quick." I pull three bags of Skittles from my backpack: regular, wild berry, and sour. Not the tropical flavor she hates. "I brought you these."

"You're bribing me?"

"It can be either. If you want to talk to me, they're just an apology gift. If you're still mad and ignoring me, then, yes, they're a bribe." I shake the bags. "So?"

She rolls her eyes before grabbing the regular and wild berry. "Keep the sour ones. I don't need my tongue burned before Saturday's competition."

"Right! I should have thought of that. Maybe we can get the competition to eat them. Send them a whole bunch of sour Skittles before the match. They won't be able to answer a single question because their tongues will be sore."

Daniela lets out a small laugh, and I reach for her hand.

"I'm so sorry."

"I don't have time for this right now, Margie. We have practice."

"Please! I'll be fast. I just need to explain. Not to make excuses, but I get it now. I got so obsessed with the dress code that I ignored that Quiz Bowl was your priority. It wasn't fair to ask you to be in the protest if it meant losing your chance to compete this weekend. I just didn't want to do it alone."

Daniela twists the end of her braid. I continue.

"Things felt different, too, like I was being left out. You were on the Quiz Bowl team and I was just the alternate. You and Jamiya are best friends now—"

"She's not my best friend."

"Really?"

Daniela rolls her eyes. "We're friends, yes, but it takes more than a few weeks for someone to become your *best* friend."

I smile, not able to help the geyser of joy rushing through my body.

"Excuse me. Coming through," Mr. Shao suddenly says as he balances an enormous slice of pizza on top of a teetering pile of copies. I open the door for him (he doesn't bother to say thank you) and then close it quickly. I need just a few more minutes.

"What was I saying? Right. You don't get a best friend that fast, but it felt like we were growing apart, like we weren't going to be the Queens of Quiz anymore, and I...I was afraid to do the protest by myself."

"It was your wild idea," Daniela says, crossing her arms.

"It was my idea, and that was part of the problem. I made the whole protest about me and what I wanted, and I didn't think about the risks for you or Jamiya or Gloria. I get it now, what you said about me not getting in trouble. Girls aren't treated fairly at our school, but girls of color are treated even worse."

"Yeah, I know," Daniela says as she rolls her eyes, and I reach for her hand again.

"No! I didn't mean you didn't know. I just meant that I finally get what you've been saying all along. I need to think about how my actions affect other people, and how if I want to make things better at our school, I need to make sure everyone's voices are included."

Daniela twists her finger around the end of her braid.

"Oh, and Gloria told me that she and the other girls got out of ISS today. Mr. Franklin canceled their suspensions and even invited them to a meeting to hear their points of view. He told her she should run for Student Council."

"I am."

"What?"

Daniela smiles. "I signed up with Ms. Anthony two weeks ago when this whole protest thing was really getting started. I told you there is more than one way to change things."

"I will totally vote for you."

She smiles, and I let go of the breath I didn't realize I was holding.

"I am really sorry."

"I know," Daniela says, letting go of my hand. "But now we have to get to practice."

"Right. Queens of Quiz."

She shakes her head. "Not yet, but we will be. And even if we're not the Queens of Quiz, we're still best friends. That's cool, too."

I smile, grabbing my backpack off the floor and following her into Mr. Shao's room.

chapter 26

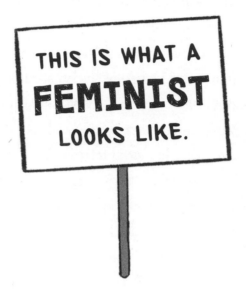

On Friday, Daniela and I race down the hallway with our lunch trays, headed to Mr. Franklin's first sixth-grade student forum in the library. No one knows what's actually going to happen when we get there, but during the announcements this morning he invited all students wanting to talk about the dress code to the library during their lunch period. Ms. Scott turned it into a "learning opportunity" and made us all look up "forum" in the dictionary.

Of course, Daniela already knew since government structures are part of her skills.

Down the hall, more students climb up the stairs with the same blue tickets we have in our hands. Anyone wanting to come had to get a ticket from the security guard in the cafeteria to make sure we didn't try to skip lunch. We probably could have taken our ticket and gone anywhere, but Daniela and I want to be in the library today.

"Ask me one more quick question before we go in," Daniela says, and I respond, "Dates of major US wars."

"American Revolutionary War, 1775 to 1783, War of 1812..."

I open the door to the library. There are so many kids inside. At the front is a huge TV screen with a PowerPoint titled LIVE OAK STUDENT FORUM in bold white letters on a blue background. Mr. Franklin is standing by the screen shuffling some papers. We wave to Jamiya, who is scanning books on the shelves with a little scan gun. All the tables are filled up except the one next to Mr. Franklin. It's mostly girls, definitely over half, but still lots of boys.

Over by the computers, Xavier sits with some boys I don't recognize.

"Should we sit up front?" Daniela asks, scanning the library for any other seats. "We might not want to be..."

"He knows, remember?"

"Right. Up front it is, then."

Daniela and I sit side by side at a table just to the left of the screen where we can see the entire room. Normally everyone would be talking and laughing and checking their phones under the table, but we all watch Mr. Franklin. A few kids are eating, but most seem to feel like me. Too excited to eat. The girls at the table across from us start to whisper, their eyes on us. It's no secret anymore that Daniela and I were the protest creators.

"Give me five," Mr. Franklin says, lifting his arm high above his head, our signal to raise our own hands and be ready to listen. He clears his throat a few times. Unlike fifth grade, everyone raises their hands right away and soon the room is silent. We're not better behaved now; we're just ready for answers.

"Thank you for joining me today in our first

student forum. We're going to have these once a month until the end of school to make sure students feel their voices are heard, by me. Your principal. Mr. Franklin."

We all stare at him, waiting. He clicks for the next slide, but nothing happens. He mutters something about technology before going to the computer and pushing the forward button himself. CIVIC ENGAGEMENT AND SOCIAL RESPONSIBILITY appear in the same white letters.

Mr. Franklin clears his throat again. "As you know, some students had a disagreement about the dress code and took actions this week that did not fit with our school policy of civic engagement"—he gestures toward the screen—"and social responsibility. Today I would like to talk to you about these two valuable skills."

Out of the corner of my eye I see a hand shoot up in the back of the room. I can't see who it is because they're blocked by a girl, Sulema, from my math class.

"Um, yes, you in the back," Mr. Franklin says. Up pops a petite Latina girl with two long black braids that go down to her waist. She adjusts her purple glasses before speaking. "Are you going to tell us why our school's dress code is sexist to girls?"

Ten hands shoot up around the room. I look at Daniela with wide eyes, and she tries to hide her smile.

"We will talk about the dress code situation after—"

Five more hands shoot up.

"Yes, you in the pink," Mr. Franklin says, stretching his neck side to side.

A white girl from my soccer league a few years ago, Kate or Katie, stands up.

"It seems like the dress code is only enforced against girls because we get in trouble for skirts and shorts, but boys don't."

More hands go up. At the table next to us a girl is bouncing in her seat, extending her arm higher and higher.

Mr. Franklin flicks to his next slide. DRESS CODE.

"Live Oak's dress code is intended to create a safe learning environment for all students—"

The room erupts. Students start whispering: "No way." "Not for girls!" "He just thinks that because..."

I lock eyes with Jamiya across the room. She mouths, "This is awesome" before returning a book to the shelf. Daniela nudges me. "You started a revolution."

"We did. This is amazing. Look at Mr. Franklin."

His round cheeks are turning red, and he brushes away the sweat collecting on his forehead. I wonder what will happen when Jamiya, Gloria, and the other eighth-grade girls show up for their forum. They have three years of anger ready to release on him.

"We will be reviewing the dress code policy to see if corrections need to be made," Mr. Franklin continues, flipping his slide to STUDENT VOICE—GET INVOLVED. It lists joining Student Council, putting suggestions in the box in the office, telling a teacher. I guess he didn't want to add "protest march" to the list.

At the table across from us, a Black girl with a clarinet in front of her holds a hand up in quiet determination. Her eyes drill into Mr. Franklin, daring him to call on her.

"We don't have time to discuss changes to the dress code now, but I invite you all to review the list of ways to get involved." Mr. Franklin looks at the crowd of lions as if he feels more and more like a gazelle. He tosses a steak into the crowd.

"I'll take one more question. Yes, you with the clarinet."

The girl stands, her hands on her clarinet case. "Mr. Franklin, I'm Naomi Davis and I want to know how you are going to address the fact that the dress code is unfair to girls, yes, but specifically biased toward girls of color. My neighbor told me that only certain girls got suspended during the protest, and that isn't right."

That was exactly my question two days ago! I wonder if he has a better answer this time. We wait, circling closer to our prey.

"The dress code has the same requirements for all girls, regardless of skin color."

Naomi's hand is back up, stretching even higher this time.

"Yes, Naomi."

"The words might be the same, but who gets in trouble and how often—that's what I'm talking about. That's prejudice and discrimination."

More hands are up around the room.

"That's something we will take into consideration as an administrative team. We want to be sure that all teachers and staff are enforcing the dress code equally."

"But what are *you* going to do about it?" someone calls from the back, and the room grumbles like a giant waking up from a centuries-long sleep. Soon students are calling out questions from all around the room.

"Will students be able to dress according to their gender identity and not what's listed in the school records?"

"What about hoodies?"

"The choir uniforms are sexist: dresses for girls and suits for boys. What about nonbinary kids? Why don't we have a gender-neutral option?"

"What's wrong with leggings? Why do we have to wear a skirt or dress over them?"

"I can't answer questions if you're all talking at once," Mr. Franklin says, trying to shout over the crowd. Their questions are like helium to our original protest, expanding it, filling it up, lifting it higher than it did when I only thought about the dress code as boys versus girls. I hadn't thought about the ways the dress code harmed all these different people. I bet Mr. Franklin is realizing the same thing. If I really want to be an activist, I'm going to have to do a lot more listening.

Buzzzzzz, the bell rings, and Mr. Franklin sighs before jumping into principal mode.

"Put your lunch trays in the large trash bins beside the door! Push your chairs in! Jason, pick that up!"

As the students file out of the library, I look at Mr. Franklin's screen. STUDENT VOICE—GET INVOLVED. Seems to me we already are.

chapter 27

The overhead lights are off in Ms. Scott's room, but sunlight still streams in from her open windows. The door was open so I didn't knock. Ms. Scott sits at her computer, pop music playing loudly on her speaker, as she flips through a stack of papers on her lap and glances at her screen. Her lips move along to a song, and her black pumps tap the tile floor.

"Ms. Scott," I call as I step into the room, my hand

brushing the tulle of my perfect first-day-of-school skirt. I changed in the bathroom after school before coming here. I only have a few minutes before practice, but I have to do this.

"Tutoring has been canceled for the day," she says, her eyes still on the paper in front of her. "I've got an appointment."

She grabs a Diet Coke beside her and looks up. "Margie?"

"I'm not here for tutoring."

"I didn't assume so. I just put your grade in, and you've got an A."

Ms. Scott takes a sip of the soda, her eyes surveying me. She sets it down and shuffles the papers on her lap. Somehow, standing in front of Ms. Scott, I don't feel as brave as I did marching in the hallway. Maybe because I wasn't alone then. Maybe because we were yelling the hard questions out into the world instead of saying them in a quiet classroom.

"Did you need something?" Ms. Scott asks. She pops the lid back on her red pen and sets it on the papers.

"I have to ask you a question. About the first day of school."

Ms. Scott crinkles her nose. "I'll do my best, but that was weeks ago."

My skirt should jump-start her memory. I step between the desks so she can see all three of its perfect tulle layers.

"Why did you dress code me that day?"

Ms. Scott smiles an exasperated smile. "Because you were out of dress code." She tips her head toward my skirt. "As evidenced by the skirt you're wearing now. Even you can see how short it is."

"But it's not that short," I say, confidence flowing up my spine like mercury in a thermometer. "I just have long legs, so it looks short."

"And yet the school handbook says differently."

"But you don't follow all the school handbook rules. You let people chew gum, and that's not allowed. Why did you care so much about my skirt?"

"I don't care about your clothing choices," she says, taking another swig of her Diet Coke. "I care about the learning that happens in my classroom.

When people are out of dress code, it disrupts other people's learning."

"I don't think that's true," I say, squeezing my hands into fists. "No one cared about my skirt. You hadn't even started teaching yet. The only person's learning that was disrupted was mine."

Ms. Scott glances at her clock. "Disagreeing with the dress code, Margaret, doesn't mean it shouldn't apply to you. Those are the rules."

"But they shouldn't be."

"Margie," Ms. Scott says, setting her hands in her lap and giving me that all-knowing teacher look. "I get it. I used to be like you—worried about my hair and my clothes. Constantly trying to impress other people, the boys I liked. But that's not what matters. What you *know* matters. What you can do with your *brain* matters."

"But I wasn't worried about those things. I just really like the skirt." I still do. It gives me the same boost of confidence I felt walking into Live Oak on the first day. "And isn't the school saying my brain doesn't matter if wearing this skirt means I have to spend the day in ISS, where I don't learn anything?"

"You'll understand better when you're older," Ms. Scott says, grabbing her red pen. "Until then, you'll just have to accept things the way they are."

For now. She doesn't know the plans we have for our next meeting with Mr. Franklin. Jamiya found a sample dress code from a school in Oregon. There, kids can wear anything as long as it covers all their private body parts and doesn't have offensive words or images of drugs, alcohol, or violence. We're hoping he might adopt the code for our school and maybe the entire school district. Ms. Scott's body-shaming rules might be the way it is now, but not for long.

I smile as I walk out of her classroom, knowing that our school will change, even if Ms. Scott doesn't.

The entire Quiz Bowl team huddles around the two practice tables while Marcus paces in front like a football coach at halftime. Daniela sits next to Jamiya, and I pull up a chair so I'm nearby. It still stings that I don't have a real seat at the table, but next year. Next year.

"This is it," Marcus says, slamming his hand

down next to a buzzer. "Go time. We get a second chance with Cactus Canyon—"

"And with Wonder Boy, the team of one from Austin Day School," Mikey adds. Everyone groans. No one can stand that four of our players got crushed by one single brain. An enormous brain, but still, just one.

"Exactly!" Marcus continues. "This is our chance to regain dominance on the Central Texas Quiz Bowl stage and to qualify for nationals. We want to start the official season with a win! We want people to know they need to watch out for Live Oak Quiz Bowl."

Beside me, Jamiya snaps a photo on her phone. I bet her caption for Instagram will make our huddle seem less desperate. Daniela turns and offers me a handful of Skittles. I scoop out the purple and reds and hand them back to her. She smiles.

"We can. Not. Lose," Marcus says, his look so intimidating that Xavier practically slides under the table.

"Enough speeches!" Mr. Shao calls from his desk. He's snacking on a really brown banana that looks like it would be 100 percent mush. "You all have an actual chance of winning this season, so let's spend time preparing for tomorrow."

Marcus walks back to the podium and pulls out a clipboard. Mikey sits on the edge of a table. "Today we have to practice strategically. No questions we already know. No categories we're familiar with. We've got to practice to win. Do we know who they're going to play for their A team?"

"It's the same four boys in all their Insta stories for the past week," Jamiya says, holding her phone out to show Mikey. He nods.

"Should be the same as our scrimmage," Marcus says.

"It is," Jamiya and Mikey answer.

"Then we need to mix it up," Marcus says, setting the clipboard down on the podium and pointing to Elman. "You're out, dude. And you, too, Jamiya."

"Excuse me?" she says, setting her phone on her lap. "If we're out, you two are. You were part of the team that lost."

Marcus shakes his head as if she's a sweet little darling. "You know Mikey and I are always on the team. We know everything."

"Not everything," I say, and all heads turn to me. Daniela's mouth drops open, and I whisper, "Trust me."

The Kings are right. They know more answers than I can imagine. But they don't know *everything*. I reach into my backpack and grab my notebook with the audit from the scrimmage. I also grab my phone, quickly opening Instagram and the Cactus Canyon Quiz Bowl feed. I show the picture to Jamiya. "These guys are the A team, right?"

She nods. Mikey and Marcus edge closer, and all the other boys lean in. I give my phone to Daniela. "Hold this up for me, please."

I flip to the right page in my notebook and point at the first Cactus Canyon student, an Asian boy with a toothy smile. "He's their pop culture guy. He knew all contemporary music, but also movies and a bit of political trivia. Not important policies or anything, but silly things that made the news. Like President Obama wearing a tan suit. This kid"—I point to a bulky white boy who looks like he could already play high school football—"knew all their chemistry and biology, plus a ton about literature. He answered every poetry or theater question." Marcus nods while Jamiya follows along on her phone. "The boy in the cougar T-shirt had geography and history, and the one whose face is sort of cut off knew everything else. He's like Everything But the...ice cream from Ben & Jerry's."

I sit back in my chair, feeling my face flush. Daniela hands back my phone and gives my hand a squeeze.

"Okay, Dress Code," Mikey says. "Who do we need?"

"I need a minute." Everyone sighs, but Daniela puts a hand on my shoulder.

"Ignore them. Do you really know all this?"

I smile. "I had to keep myself busy somehow as an alternate."

"Planning a protest wasn't enough?"

I laugh, ripping out a page and handing it to Daniela. "Will you help me?"

While the boys around us go back to video games on their phones, Jamiya scoots over a chair so she can watch over Daniela's shoulder.

"What is all that?" she asks, and I hold up a finger while I scan pages.

"Okay," I tell Daniela, finally finding the right page. "List the names of everyone on the team." One by one I list the strengths of each person. Marcus and Mikey each have seven true strengths (I'm not listing any lucky answers), but most of the other boys only have three or four. We get to Jamiya, and I list "world religions, chemistry lab techniques, African American civil rights leaders, and general music and dance."

"Add Brexit and political symbols," Jamiya says with a smile. "I've been studying those for the past two weeks."

"I can do yours," I say to Daniela, taking the pencil from her and listing the many categories my best friend knows by heart. She is meant to be a Quiz Bowl Queen. I show her the list and she nods.

"You're down to forty-five minutes and you haven't done a single round, gentlemen," Mr. Shao calls.

"And ladies," Jamiya shouts with a smirk. Daniela gives her a high five.

"We're on it, Mr. Shao!" Marcus says before turning to me. "Let's go, Dress Code."

"I'm ready." I stand up, smoothing my skirt down

and holding the paper in front of me like an acceptance speech.

"To beat Cactus Canyon, we'll need Mikey and Marcus." They shrug like "obviously." "Jamiya." She nods, crossing her arms over her chest. "And Daniela."

"You're just saying that because she's your best friend," Xavier cries, setting his phone down on the table with the video game characters still bouncing around.

"I'm not. She knows nine major categories, and honestly"—I turn to Marcus and Mikey—"if she wasn't in sixth grade and wasn't a girl, she would have been on the A team all along. This has been the boys club for a while, but that's got to stop. Didn't you see what we, the girls of Live Oak, accomplished this week?"

"Hey, I marched," Xavier pipes up.

"Whether you're doing it on purpose or not, you don't always give the girls on the team an equal shot. We're going to keep losing if we don't use all the assets we have."

"Might be worth it to listen to her," Mr. Shao says, spinning around in his chair, the banana peel now stacked on some papers beside him. He gives me a thumbs-up before popping his headphones over his ears, and I wonder how much he's been paying attention while we all thought he wasn't listening.

I point to Daniela. "She studies way more than anyone." I put a hand up. "Except you, Mikey. And she knows math better than anyone in the room."

"Math is my category," Elman says, and I sigh.

"Are you going to let me finish?"

"Everyone, hush up!" Marcus says, leaning against the desk. "So you're saying we're unfair to the girls on the team?"

"You have been."

Mikey turns to Jamiya. "Do you think that's true?"

She pauses. "Honestly, yes. I know you did a lot this year to get more representation for black and brown kids on the team, and that's awesome, seriously, but there are only three girls on this team, and ten boys. We're doing something wrong if our numbers are so uneven."

"Maybe girls just don't want to be on Quiz Bowl," Elman says, and a few others echo his feeling.

Jamiya sighs as I answer. "They won't want to be part of Quiz Bowl if they feel like it's a place girls aren't welcome."

Mikey nods. "I get that. We can do better."

"But can we talk about this after practice?" Marcus says, shifting his feet. "You girls don't want to lose, either."

"Of course not, but this conversation is far from over."

"Understood, Dress Code."

Jamiya and I give him a look. "Understood, *Margie*," he says. "Back to teams: we need me, Mikey, Jamiya, and Daniela?"

"Yes. To beat Cactus Canyon. But to beat Mateo from Austin Day School you need Mikey, Jamiya, Daniela, and"—I take a deep breath—"me."

Shouts of "No!" and "Seriously?" fill the room.

"You?" Jamiya asks, and I nod.

"I couldn't believe we lost to a team of one, so I've been watching all the old YouTube videos of his matches. His mom posts them on the Austin Day School channel. She even has practice sessions filmed and these 'Are you smarter than a sixth grader?' episodes. I know how he plays. He's quick to buzz in on the topics he doesn't know well, but he actually buzzes in slowly when he's confident. Like he has all the time in the world. I think I can help us beat him."

And I mean that. I can help, but I can't do it alone.

Marcus and Mikey look at each other, sharing some sort of twin mind reading that I don't understand. Marcus shrugs and grabs his clipboard.

"Well, let's see what you got then, Margie."

chapter 28

The lights on the auditorium stage are bright, just the way I always hoped they would be. Behind a podium is the adult moderator, flipping through a stack of questions we'll soon have to answer. Three tournament officials, including the director, are seated at a table just below the stage. Dad's out there in the audience somewhere. Grandma Colleen, too, but I don't look into the crowd because I can't risk the distraction.

At the far end of the table, Mikey leans back in his chair, his arms crossed behind his head, as if he's not as terrified as the rest of us. Jamiya and Daniela mouth answers to themselves, running through different lists of facts in hopes that my predictions were right and we crammed the correct Need to Know lists.

Across from us, Mateo of Austin Day School sits chatting with his mom, who keeps pulling out little bags full of food. First, he ate strawberries. Then some pretzels. Now he's drinking Gatorade like we're under the hot Texas sun and not an over-air-conditioned auditorium. I adjust the bow Jamiya gave me, pulling my ponytail tighter.

"Good luck today!" Mateo calls from his table, and we all mutter "Thanks." Even though he could crush us again, I can't be mad at him. He seems really nice. And he's kind of cute.

The moderator takes a sip from a plastic water bottle beside the microphone on the podium and leans forward.

"Good afternoon, contestants. We're ready to begin our second match of this season opener." The crowd cheers, and someone shouts "Go, Lions!" I really wish I could see Dad giving me a thumbs-up. We beat Cactus Canyon in the first match, but now it's my turn. This is the moment I've been waiting for since I started middle school.

"Contestants," the moderator says, turning her head to look at both teams. "You've been made aware of the rules during the previous match, so we're going to begin straightaway. We also have to be out of here by five o'clock." The parents in the audience laugh. She turns to us.

"Live Oak Middle, are you ready?"

"Yes," we all answer, Daniela's voice barely a squeak.

"Austin Day School, are you ready?"

"Yes!" Mateo says, his shoulders back, his hands crossed on the table like he's waiting to speak in front of the United Nations.

"Okay," she says. "Nine minutes on the clock, and here's toss-up one."

I can barely keep up with the moderator, who is reading so fast she stumbles over some of the words. Didn't she practice? We did.

Mateo buzzes in before I can really understand what's happening. *Focus, Margie.* The second toss-up comes: "Represented by the Greek letter *phi*, this irrational number reflects—"

Buzz. The judge nods at Daniela. "The golden ratio."

"Correct. Fifteen points."

Yes! Before the power mark! Now for the bonus questions. "According to legend, this city was founded by twin brothers who argued over an auspicious location for its creation. For ten points, name this city—"

Jamiya buzzes in. "Rome."

"Correct. Ten points." *Yes!* I'm so glad we made her the captain for this round.

The second asks which god was their father. I picture the page in my Greek and Roman mythology book Dad got me for Christmas in fourth grade, when I was obsessed.

"Ares," Daniela whispers, and I shake my head. That's the Greek name.

"Mars," I call to Jamiya, and she buzzes in.

"Correct." I breathe a sigh of relief.

"As infants, Romulus and Remus were placed into a basket and sent down the Tiber River and discovered by one of these animals."

"A wolf," Mikey whispers, and Jamiya repeats it.

"Correct. That's thirty on the bonus."

The crowd breaks into applause, and I turn when Dad yells, "Go get 'em, Margie!" I scan the shadowed faces but can't see him.

Our celebration doesn't last long because Mateo beats us on the next two toss-ups and then we lose five points when Jamiya incorrectly answers a question about the Nobel Prize. Mikey leans down the table. "Relax. We got this. Remember the buzzer."

We all nod. We had practiced with both types of buzzers, the one you hold in your hand and the one that lies flat on the table. We tried different techniques for buzzing in, timing ourselves to the millisecond, knowing that to beat Mateo every moment would count. I squeeze the buzzer in my hand, resting my thumb on the bright-red button.

"Toss-up number three," the moderator says. "Another math question."

Mateo smiles, knowing math is one of his best subjects. I pat Daniela's shoulder with my free hand. He's not the only one with kick-butt math skills.

"Pencil and paper ready. Alexander needs to determine the equation for a line passing through point (-7,-4) with slope m=5. By solving first for the y-intercept, he computes—for ten points—what equation representing this line?"

Buzz. Daniela's buzzer lights up.

"$y = 5x + 31$."

"Correct. And here's your bonus." I stare above Mateo's head, giving my brain space to listen as the moderator asks us about the Burgess formation. We get the first and second questions about its composition correct ("fossils" and "shale"), but misidentify its location (Canada, not Alaska), leaving us down fifty points.

"Some slang terms for this offense include 'wagging' in Britain or 'playing hooky' in the United States. A result of compulsory education laws, what offense—"

Mateo beats us to the buzzer. "Truancy."

"That is correct." His mom and family cheer,

and he beams. There's no way that boy has been truant once in his life. Though people probably thought I wasn't a rule breaker, either, and here I am, #codebreaker.

We lose the next few toss-ups, and I can feel this win pulling away from us. I don't dare look in the audience where Marcus is sitting, not participating. I convinced them that we, the girls, could do this. That we were the only ones who could take down Mateo, but the first half is almost over and we're still down by almost a hundred and fifty points.

Finally, the timer beeps and the moderator calls the end of the first half. During our three-minute break, we pull our chairs closer to Mikey. He rubs a hand across his face, his cool dissipating like dry ice.

"How is he still beating us?"

"He hasn't answered a single toss-up wrong," Daniela says with a sigh.

"It's actually a good thing that he's winning by so many points," I argue.

"Excuse me?" Jamiya asks, and I nod.

"Remember? He buzzes in slower when he's

confident. Right now, he thinks he can beat us. He's relaxing already. Look."

Mateo is snacking on blue-and-pink cotton candy in a ziplock bag, handed over by his mom. He sips some Gatorade and waves at us.

"You guys are doing really good this time! A few toss-ups with the bonus and we're tied."

His smile would annoy me if he was being sarcastic, but he's not. He's just as sweet as that cotton candy.

"We can take him in this next round," Mikey says, leaning forward to rest his forearms on his knees. "We take him down while he's confident, and then we just don't stop. Your plan better work, Dress—Margie."

I take a deep breath. "It's not about my plan anymore. It's about us. We can do this."

Jamiya nods and Daniela squeezes my hand. How hard can it be to defeat one boy?

The second half of the match flies by with my fingers slamming the buzzer so fast my thumb has a red mark. With each answer—Bay of Bengal, Plato, a red square—we move faster than Mateo, and our rising score gets to him. Soon, he's perched up in his chair, legs tucked underneath him, elbows resting on top of the table. He bites his lower lip, occasionally closing his eyes as he listens to each question.

With less than three minutes on the board, we're only down by forty-five points. "Toss-up number twenty. Males of this species utilize a brood pouch to incubate their offspring—"

I watch Mateo move in milliseconds, the words channeling from our ear canals into the Wernicke area and the angular gyrus, flying through our neurons and synapses and headed straight to our thumbs. In slow motion, I watch his thumb bend, slamming my buzzer down at the same time.

My buzzer lights up red. "Seahorse."

"Correct. Fifteen points." On to the bonus. Mateo's head drops, his dark hair flopping over his eyes. I look away.

"For ten points each—answer the following about technological developments to the television. Appropriately called the Lazy Bones, the first television remote communicated with the television set in what manner?"

"Radio waves?" Mikey suggests, and Jamiya shakes her head.

"Infrared light?" Daniela adds, and again Jamiya shakes her head.

"What, then?" Mikey huffs.

"I'm thinking," Jamiya says.

"Team, we need an answer."

"Wires," Jamiya answers, and Mikey slumps back in his chair. *What was she thinking?*

"Correct. Ten points."

Jamiya smiles. "You've got to trust me." I don't know when she added midcentury technology to her studies, but I'm glad she did. Daniela smashes the next question about infrared, and Mikey scores ten for "analog." We're tied up!

"You guys are really heating up," Mateo calls before the moderator reads the next question. I smile, wanting to trounce him and also, maybe, be his friend. He could lose this match, but he's still smiling.

Mateo gets the next question on the Ottoman

Empire, but only at a ten-point level. Then, he misses one of the bonuses. His mom shouts encouragement. Our crowd is silent. We're down by thirty points, and the timer just passed twenty seconds. "This American mathematician's calculations of orbital mechanics contributed to the success of the first US crewed spaceflights. Her role at NASA—"

Jamiya beats Mateo to the buzzer. We wait. A nod. "Katherine Johnson."

"Correct. Fifteen points."

The crowd erupts, but we still have to nail two bonus questions to win. Mateo drops his head to the table before picking it up with a smile. "We got this," Jamiya whispers. "Just take our time and stay calm."

The timer beeps, signaling the end of the match. Thankfully, we get the next three bonus questions anyway. "This daughter of a tenant farmer at Domrémy believed herself guided by divine voices—"

"Joan of Arc," Daniela and I call at the exact same time. I press a hand to my shirt, feeling beneath it my pendant with Joan of Arc carrying a flag, the words PRAY FOR US inscribed below. Jamiya calmly repeats our answer to the moderator.

"Correct. Joan of Arc led the French army to a massive victory at this city during the Hundred Years' War."

Mikey points to us. "You guys got this."

I shake my head. "Daniela does."

"Orléans," she tells Jamiya, even pronouncing it the proper French way, not *Or-leens*, as Dad says. Jamiya repeats her answer and the moderator nods.

"Correct. Ten points."

Our side of the crowd erupts. That's it. We did it.

"And for the final points of tonight's match. Despite being falsely described by early historians as a mere "cheerleader" for the French army, Joan of Arc carried this medieval weapon into battle."

Daniela smiles. "A lance."

We don't hear the moderator proclaim "correct" over the cheers of the crowd. The rest of the Quiz Bowl team rushes the stage, their arms and hands pulling us up and out of chairs as the group laughs and high fives.

Across from us, Mateo's mom places her hand on his shoulder, and he pauses to tidy up the buzzers at his solitary table. When we lock eyes, he gives me a thumbs-up. Suddenly, Daniela pulls me into a big hug, her jumping feet lifting us off the stage floor.

"We did it!"

We did. Joan of Arc may not have ended the Hundred Years' War, but she led the charge. We may not have ended sexism at our school, but we gave it a start. We're code breakers. Change makers. And soon, the Queens of Quiz.

ACKNOWLEDGMENTS

The road to publication for my debut novel was five or more years, so I'm still amazed at how quickly *Margie Kelly Breaks the Dress Code* is out in the world. So many people helped make it possible, especially:

My editor, Nikki Garcia, who has been a consistent guide, always asking the right questions to push this story where I wanted it to go. You give me confidence my books will be good, even when I'm deep in the stages of revision and it all seems like trash. Editing this book will always be part of the strange memories of April 2020, when we were both staying home and staying safe as the world battled COVID-19. I'm forever grateful for the distraction of escaping with you into the world of books.

My agent, Melissa Edwards, who supports my ideas while still reining them in. I'm so grateful for your constant advocacy and the way you'll always send the email I don't want to write.

My WriteByNight book coach, Jessamine Chan: you were a constant cheerleader, and the only person who has read all the variations of this book. (Remember when Margie stole the ball at a powder-puff football game?) You even managed to keep up with all the changing character names. I'm grateful for your willingness to support me as an author, not just as a writer, and for having the hard talks about what it means to be a white author and how that identity affects the stories I tell.

It has been a joy working with the Little, Brown Books for Young Readers team for a second time. I am always impressed by the attention to detail of my copy editors, Marisa Finkelstein and Sherri Schmidt, who uncover disregarded subplots and irregular timelines like paleontologists. Your work gives me the freedom to focus primarily on the story. Thank you. Thanks as well to Julia Bereciartu for capturing the spirit and energy of Margie Kelly and friends. It's amazing to see the characters in my head suddenly appear in front of me, and I couldn't be happier with this vibrant cover. I'm also grateful for the talents of designer Angelie Yap and my publicist, Katharine McAnarney.

Also at WriteByNight, owner Justine Duhr: your company makes my books happen. Thank you. And Tom Andes, I appreciated your perspective into the novel as you helped me see how the message I wanted to relay was still waiting to be revealed.

Ria Ferich, Natalie Neumann, and Nina Vizcar-rondo: thank you for your help with the protest signs and other feminist trivia. You're great advocates, and even better friends.

Thank you to my teacher friend, Sarah Paiga, for answering my questions about sixth-grade math and for bringing so much joy (and jalapeño dip) to our Fulmore lunches. And thank you to Beth Griesmer, another teacher colleague turned friend, who read the last-minute chapter revisions and discussed my ideas while we walked the neighborhood. I'm so glad to know you and be your friend.

Muchísima gracias, Christi Almeida, por tu ayuda

con el español y el spanglish en esta novela. Por siempre, my perfect work wife, no hay nadie mejor que tú.

Writing a book about race and gender takes insight from many people. I'm grateful to both Idris Grey and Brandy Colbert, authenticity readers at different stages of this project. Your knowledge and experience helped me write a novel that reflects the many students who will read it. Thank you. Gratitude, also, to Daniel Williams and Leslie LaFollette for your perspectives on queer identity. (And thank you, Daniel, for officiating our wedding!) So much of my educational philosophy is owed to you, Dr. Terrance Green, but thank you specifically for providing me research on the capitalization of Black (and for helping me become an anti-racist educator). I also relied heavily on the Writing with Color Tumblr—a great resource!

The idea for this book originated in the halls of Fulmore Middle School. I have learned so much from my students about their experiences of racism and sexism in school, and the many ways I, too, have played a part. I'm grateful to all my former students for sharing your stories, speaking out in the classroom or on the stage, and for giving me so much hope that the world will change for the better.

My husband, Shiva, who does all our cooking, cleaning, and gardening: you break the stereotype of gender roles and make it possible for me to spend so much time upstairs, writing. I'm grateful for your love and support, as well as your ability to come up with synonyms on demand. I love you forever.

And finally, my parents: Thank you for buying me all those Girl Power T-shirts. This book is for you. And Dad, you've always been great at shopping for me; that navy corduroy miniskirt was perfect. Despite what Coach said, you were right—it wasn't too short for school.